Andie
AND THE BOYS

Janice Harrell

AN ARCHWAY PAPERBACK
Published by POCKET BOOKS
New York   London   Toronto   Sydney   Tokyo   Singapore

AN ARCHWAY PAPERBACK *Original*

An Archway Paperback published by
POCKET BOOKS, a division of Simon & Schuster Inc.
1230 Avenue of the Americas, New York, NY 10020

ISBN: 0-671-69668-8

First Archway Paperback printing December 1990

10 9 8 7 6 5 4 3 2 1

AN ARCHWAY PAPERBACK and colophon
are registered trademarks of Simon & Schuster Inc.

Cover photo by Mort Engel
Clothes courtesy of United Colors of Benetton

Printed in the U.S.A.

IL 6+

For my mother

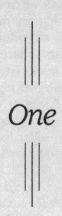

One

"Marry him!" I told my mother when she started sounding me out about Richard. "He's rich, good-looking, kind to animals, and you're not getting any younger. What are you waiting for?" I applied another dab of Carioca Pink to my toenails and surveyed my feet with satisfaction.

"It isn't as easy as you might think to blend two families, Andie. Two careers. Two lives."

"I don't see the problem." To me, Richard's house looked bigger than the average parking garage. How much blending would people have to do in a place like that?

"We'd have to move to North Carolina," Mom pointed out. "You'd have to switch to a new school. There'll be a lot of adjusting."

"You mean we'd have to adjust to not hearing

from bill collectors?" I perked up. "Don't worry about it, Mom. I think we can handle it."

I should explain that my mom is a writer. She mostly writes those adventure books with racy covers that they sell in airports. She also writes the sort of inspirational books you see on wire racks in grocery stores. Mom's writing had paid the bills since my father died, but at times it was a close squeeze. For some writers a good year is when their book makes the best-seller list. For Mom a good year is when she doesn't have to take a publisher to small claims court.

I didn't expect her to marry Richard for his money, but under the circumstances an extra income in the family would be useful.

Mom frowned at the calendar on the kitchen wall. "Too bad Richard can't afford to take off much time. It has to be Labor Day."

"What happens on Labor Day?" I guess my attention had wandered. Painting the nail of my little toe requires intense concentration.

"The wedding."

I turned around and gaped at the calendar. Mom had circled the first weekend in September with a red marker.

"Margaret Patterson said you could stay with Mindy that weekend while Richard and I take a short wedding trip to the Bahamas."

I gulped. Obviously Mom had already made up her mind to marry Richard before we had begun our cozy little chat. The wedding was set and I was practically the last one to know. The funny thing was that it was a shock. During all the time Mom had been seeing him, I realized that marriage was a possibility, but then so was atomic war and I'd never truly thought that was going to happen, either.

Mom thumbtacked a list of wedding guests to the bulletin board. I stared at it in disbelief. It was typed, clear evidence of premeditation. She chewed on her marker and studied me out of the corner of her eye. "I met some of P.J.'s gang when I was there last weekend, and one of them is really good-looking."

Right at that moment I wasn't biting. Good-looking boys were far from my mind. Basic everyday survival was what I was focusing on. I barely managed to keep the sound of panic out of my voice. "What's Richard's son like? I only met him that one time."

"P.J.? Oh, a typical teenager, I guess."

"What's that supposed to mean?"

"I don't know, Andie. Moody, difficult. But underneath he's really a nice boy. I think Richard's inclined to be a little hard on him. Richard was sort of wild as a kid, and now he drives himself crazy worrying that P.J. may do some of the stupid things he did."

"Really?" I was interested. "What sort of stupid things?"

Mom put a used tea bag down the garbage disposal and the resulting roar drowned me out. She's good at sidestepping questions.

For the record, my mom and I are not at all alike. It is purely an accident of heredity that we resemble each other. I got my good legs and auburn hair from

3

her. Also we both lose our appetite when things go wrong, which, life being what it is, keeps us thin. The significant difference between us is that I am a realist and Mom is a romantic. My mom wears flowers in her hair, listens to sad songs in French, and dreams of seeing the pyramids. She actually married a race car driver—my father. What could be more impractical than that? He departed this world in a blaze of glory during a nasty pileup in Daytona. Needless to say he carried no life insurance. I considered it a stroke of luck that this time around Mom had fallen for a respectable guy who owned a chain of department stores, because I wouldn't have put it past her to marry a stuntman, or even another writer. Compared to people in high-risk vocations like those, Richard was a good deal indeed. No matter how hard I tried, I couldn't imagine his being wild as a kid. This was a guy who excused himself after every meal to brush his teeth, the original pin-striped conformist.

Not that Richard's conformity bothered me. I'll take safety over glamour any time. I have a cautious streak a mile wide. It's not clear where I got it, since both of my parents were the exact opposite of me. In fact, it's practically unbelievable that I turned out so sensible.

I was only six when my father died. We followed him around on the race circuit when I was little, and I have all these memories of crawling around on the floor in carpeted hotel rooms with Mom's typewriter rattling nearby. I remember I liked to wrap the heavy hotel curtains around me and twirl round and round until I was wrapped up like a mummy. There aren't too many things for a little kid to do in a hotel room, I guess. One time I picked up the phone and dialed just the way I had seen my mom and dad do. "Betty's Hair Salon," a brisk voice said. I giggled nervously, feeling a wild sense of power. "Who is this!" fumed the woman. "Who *is* this?" At that point I got scared and hung up. Even today when people complain about getting phone calls from "heavy breathers," I feel faintly guilty.

It is quite possible that that one phone call at the age of four or five was about the limit of my taste for adventure. Or maybe I developed a dislike for any kind of change while I was being dragged from one strange hotel room to another during those formative years. All I could be sure of now that Mom had made her announcement was that I was shaken. I was facing nothing worse than an improvement in my standard of living, and I felt sick to my stomach.

I grabbed a cotton ball, wiped a smear of nail polish off my toe, and tried to remind myself that it was good for Mom to marry Richard. It was only that I hadn't expected the wedding to happen so soon, and now that it came down to it, I realized I was a little vague about some details that might turn out to be important.

I wished I had paid more attention that time I visited Richard's house. Taken notes, even. How much did I really know about him and his kid?

"I'm very flexible," I muttered. "I can get along with all kinds."

I was trying to boost my morale a little, but Mom

didn't seem to be listening. She was leafing through the Yellow Pages listings under Florists. As she would have put it herself, my fate was sealed.

Mom and Richard were married in a tasteful ceremony the Saturday before Labor Day. Richard saw to it that I had a knockout beige linen dress that emphasized the red in my hair and which had the welcome side effect of making me look at least eighteen. The dress was almost too good. When I thought about its price, I was afraid it might be some kind of bribe.

I glanced over at P.J., a tall skinny kid with a cowlick and the animated expression of a cigar-store Indian. At the moment he was standing at the buffet table scarfing down shrimp. I made my way over to him with the idea of sounding him out about my new home.

I cleared my throat. "So, I guess we're going to the same school now, huh?"

He grunted and stuffed a large butterfly shrimp in his mouth.

"How do you like it there? Is it pretty good?"

He shrugged. Old P.J. was not exactly turning out to be a store of information. What jolly chats we'd have once we were all living in the same house!

Richard appeared and put his hand on P.J.'s shoulder. "Did P.J. tell you that he's just turned sixteen?"

"Some birthday," P.J. muttered.

"He already passed the driving test. And I've got a car for you kids to use. We picked it out last week."

My cup of punch wobbled in my hand as I was overcome with rosy visions of mobility. I would no longer be a lowly peasant slogging along on the pavement, but one of the aristocrats. Wheels!

"I know you don't have your license yet, Andie," Richard went on, bringing me down to earth, "but don't worry about that. P.J. can do the driving until you get it. The school bus situation up on Rocky Knoll isn't the greatest, and I don't want Ellen to have to spend all her time chauffeuring you kids back and forth. She's got her work to think about."

P.J. stared at the floral arrangement on the buffet table with such intensity that I expected the carnations to burst into flames. It was pretty obvious that he had been counting on having the new car all to himself. Too bad. I wasn't about to give up my share of it just to please him. After all, Richard had distinctly said that the car was for both of us, and it was clear I was going to need the transportation.

When Richard sauntered off to greet more guests, I made another effort to get information out of P.J.

"Is the driving test in North Carolina hard?" I asked. My sixteenth birthday was coming up in a couple of months, and I had been getting kind of anxious about the test.

"It's a piece of cake. It's just the way it was when we went over it in driver's ed."

"I never took it. Mom taught me to drive."

"You've got to have driver's ed. to get a license in North Carolina," he said flatly. "You can't even get a *learner's* permit until you've had driver's ed."

My whole life flashed before my eyes. My blood

ran cold. "You mean, I'm not going to be able to get a license?"

"I can't believe this. No, you can't get a license. Unreal! I guess I'm supposed to take you everywhere. Great. Terrific."

We stared at each other in mutual distrust for a moment.

"There you are, sweetheart!" Mom suddenly threw her arms around me and squeezed me tight. "We're off. Have a good time at Mindy's," she said breathlessly.

Mom was leaving! I had almost forgotten about that part of it—she and Richard were off to the Bahamas. I couldn't even cry on Mom's shoulder now. I was supposed to be happy for her.

Just then someone handed me a bag of rice tied with pink ribbons. I noticed then that people were pressing toward the door. Mom and Richard were smiling insanely at each other as they made their way toward the door.

Somehow my friends Mindy and Lianne managed to find me in the crowd. Maybe they had followed the sound of sniffling. "Your stepbrother is so cute," Mindy said. "I've always wanted to have a brother. I bet he'll introduce you to lots of neat boys."

Horns blared outside. Someone yelled, "Bon voyage!" I realized that Mom and Richard were driving away and I still hadn't thrown my bag of rice. It didn't seem to matter. I blew my nose loudly.

When I glanced over at the buffet table I saw that P.J., his expression bleak, had broken open his package of rice and was dropping it into the punch bowl grain by grain.

"We'll write you." Mindy hugged me. "And Westmarket's not that far away, really. Five hours' drive."

"Six," put in Lianne, glumly.

Westmarket didn't seem just six hours away from Washington, D.C. to me, now. It seemed like a different universe. I wished Grouman's Department Stores hadn't opened a branch in D.C. Then Richard would never have come here and met Mom and we would be staying at home where we belonged. Suddenly I wanted to grab hold of my two best friends and never let go. I wanted to lash myself to the banisters of my old school. I saw it all so clearly. I would move in with Mindy and support myself by selling my special gumbo-vegetable soup which I make by mixing a can of chicken gumbo soup with a can of vegetable soup.

Mindy sighed. "It was a beautiful wedding. Don't you just love weddings?"

She had not picked the right moment to ask me.

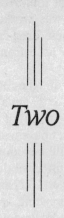

TWO

When Mom and Richard picked me up at Mindy's after the honeymoon, it seemed as if they were trailing confetti. Not that there were actually bits of it falling out of their pockets, but the air of festivity that hovered over them told me they were completely out of touch with reality—like that the next day I was starting in a new school where I didn't know a soul. Unless you counted P.J., and I didn't.

During the six-hour drive to Westmarket I asked forty or fifty pertinent questions. "Don't worry about a thing," Richard kept saying. "P.J. can show you around."

We pulled into town just before six. "Maybe we could just drive by the school," I suggested, "and take a look at it."

"Oh, sweetheart, it's so late." Mom stretched her

legs awkwardly. "Let's just get some supper. After all, you'll be seeing it tomorrow morning."

My imagination was working overtime. Fully functioning dungeons, drug-crazed ninjas—what were they trying to hide from me? "Just a little peek?" I pleaded.

"It's practically on the other side of town, Andie," Richard said. "That's part of what makes the bus situation so bad, that and the shortage of bus drivers. You won't have to deal with any of that, though, because you'll be riding with P.J."

The car climbed up a winding road past a gate that said "Rocky Knoll." It came to rest in front of Richard's house, sprawling across a bluff. It had been attractively landscaped with junipers, geraniums, roses, rail fences, lanterns, and all the other little touches that God would have put there in the first place if only he had had the money.

Richard pulled into the garage, looked around, and registered disappointment. "P.J. must still be out with his friends. Oh, well, I guess we can handle these boxes ourselves. There isn't that much."

We spent the next hour unpacking the U-Haul trailer and carting Mom's and my worldly possessions to the upstairs bedrooms. The house was on three levels, great practice for mountain climbing, but not so great for moving in. After the fourth trip up to my bedroom, I was grateful that years of budgeting had left me short of possessions. I staggered up the stairs for what seemed an eternity carrying boxes while sweat trickled between my shoulder blades. I began to understand how Richard managed to keep his youthful figure. The layout of the house was better than a health club membership. It was the kind of place where if you left your comb upstairs you'd just buy a new one.

When we had the boxes unloaded, I went down to the car for one last check around. I found a couple of tapes that had spilled out, also my favorite ball-point pen. My teddy bear Finnegan sat patiently on the back seat of the car, waiting for me. I retrieved him and gave him a quick hug.

Just then I heard a whirring noise overhead. The garage door rose. P.J. drove straight toward me in a shiny red Camaro and stuck his head out the window. "I saw the lights and thought I'd better check in. Tell Dad I'll be back in a minute. I've got to run the guys home."

Suddenly the front passenger door of the Camaro flew open and long legs slid out. When the owner of the legs got out and stood up to his full height, I saw his blond hair gleaming like candlelight. His incredible smile just about knocked me senseless.

"Hey, we don't want to run off before we get introduced, do we?" He walked up to me and put his arm around me. "Hi, Andie. I'm Chris." His breath smelled of pizza.

I wished I wasn't holding Finnegan. I was definitely at risk of dropping him on account of my knees turning wobbly and unreliable.

"Get out, Dooley," Chris yelled, "and say hello to P.J.'s new sister!"

Dooley pushed the seat forward and got out. Then he leaned against the side of the car, melancholy black eyes staring out at me from a sallow face. More than anything, Dooley looked like one of the Borgias, that Renaissance family famous for dipping poisoned rings into their enemies' wine cups. "Hi," he said in a froggy voice.

I hesitated. "Hi," I said.

"Come on, you guys," said P.J. "I don't have all night. My dad's probably up there pitching a fit right now."

Dooley dropped into the back seat as if pulled by invisible elastic. Chris raised his hand in a mute salute and slid back into the car. P.J. revved up the engine. A second later the Camaro backed out of the garage and roared away.

I took Finnegan upstairs to my room and put him on the bed. I was still a little shaky from Chris's touch. In the past few minutes I had been forced to reevaluate all the boys I had ever known and had moved each of them down a notch. Chris was definitely at the top. And to think that he was already showing an interest in me! I considered it a good omen. It was almost as if I had seen a rainbow over the house. Unfortunately, a little voice inside me, the realistic one, took over and told me that P.J. was bound to figure out some way to ruin it all for me.

I was pretty shook, and being in a totally new place was not helping any. I looked around the big room and realized that the wide open spaces made me want to hide under the bed. I didn't like the way my feet sank ankle deep into the carpet. It was possible I was not cut out for a life of luxury.

I propped Finnegan up on the white candlewick bedspread and went downstairs to look for Mom and Richard. The large family room and the attached kitchen had an entire wall of windows that looked out over a wide creek far below. Currently a sunset was turning the creek pink. The view was undeniably pretty, but the whole room felt like a photo for *Architectural Digest,* not like home. There was only one familiar thing about it—the smell.

"I can't believe P.J. hasn't taken out the garbage." Richard had come into the room and was pulling a plastic trash container out from under the sink. He stared at it with the unhealthy fascination most people reserve for road accidents.

"I'll take it out," I said.

"No, no, Andie, you don't have to do that."

"I like taking out garbage." A lie, but as a newcomer to the house, I figured I needed all the brownie points I could get. I took the bag from him, recoiling a little from the stench.

"It goes out behind the garage," he said. "I'll switch on the lights out back for you. It's starting to get dark." He frowned. "I wonder where P.J. can be."

"I meant to tell you. He drove in a minute ago. He's just going to run his friends home, and then he'll be right back."

"He knew when we'd be getting in." Richard scowled. "He should have been here."

"Ri-chard," Mom yodeled from the stairway. "Where do you keep your light bulbs?"

Holding the plastic bag at arm's length, I made my way downstairs to the garage. I nudged open the door at the back of the garage and found the garbage cans, which for aesthetic reasons had been concealed by a low wooden fence. Everything in

Richard's neighborhood seemed to be aesthetic, even garbage. After I dumped the bag, I stood by the cans catching a picture postcard view of the broad creek below and feeling deeply and painfully homesick for urban decay.

"Greetings!"

I whirled around and saw a girl sitting on the fence under an oak tree at the edge of the lot.

"I'm Rachel Green, your next-door neighbor. Are you just moving in? Or are you here for a long visit or something? I saw your trailer driving up. Does P.J. know you're here? I saw him driving away, so I guess he doesn't know you've come, huh?"

She talked so fast that her words tumbled over one another. I didn't have a chance to answer one question before she shot out another.

"We're living here now," I said. "My mom just married P.J.'s dad. I'm Andie Baker."

"You're here for good? Ooo, super!" She flashed a dazzling expanse of white teeth so that for a second I had the weird sensation I was talking to the Cheshire cat. She was wearing a painter's hat, and under it I could make out the glint of her glasses. She was also wearing some kind of baggy T-shirt. Her long skinny legs were wrapped around the rail fence. "You can't imagine how neat it's going to be to have a girl up on the knoll," she said. "I mean there isn't one single girl up here who's past tricycle age. If you hadn't shown up, I would have had to start playing with My Little Ponies."

I heard the Camaro's motor. "I guess I'd better go," I said. "I can tell that P.J.'s back."

"It's going to be blissful to have another civilized being on the bus," she added quickly. "I mean, there are all these creepy guys on the bus that hold cigarette lighters under your hand and drop books on your head, but now that there are two of us, we can watch each other's backs and band together for survival." She scrunched up her shoulders and grinned at me.

"I'm going to be riding to school with P.J." If I had had any thought of giving the bus a try, Rachel's information about the boys with cigarette lighters finished it.

"Oh."

"Well, see ya." Feeling like a traitor to my sex, I left her sitting forlornly on the fence. I had my own troubles. I wasn't in any shape to do social work.

As I mounted the stairs I could hear raised voices from the kitchen. I slowed my steps and whistled a few tuneless bars to tell them I was coming. I didn't want to walk in with Richard in full roar.

P.J. and Richard both stared at me when I stepped in the kitchen door. They looked as if they had forgotten I lived there. That was understandable. I kept forgetting it myself. For the first time I noticed how much they looked alike—same dark eyebrows, same red veins in bulging eyeballs.

Richard glared at P.J. "And you can take that last box upstairs too."

"I don't even know where to put it."

"Andie can show you."

"Oh, sure," I said quickly. "Sure I can." As far as I was concerned, the sooner the combatants were separated the better.

P.J. shot me a resentful look as he hoisted the box and headed for the stairs. I followed him up. "Jeez, a guy could get a hernia carrying this," he complained. "What's in here? Gold bricks?"

"Books."

"You say books?"

"One reads them," I explained. "For fun and profit."

"Jeez."

He dumped them unceremoniously at the door to my room. The panes in the window at the end of the hall rattled in sympathy.

"I just met the girl who lives next door," I said.

He looked at me uncomprehendingly.

"Rachel Green."

"Oh, yeah. She lives next door."

"Well, thanks for bringing up the books."

He began to walk away, but suddenly stopped and turned around. He leaned one shoulder against the wall and frowned angrily at me. "Look, Andie, I just want to clue you in on one thing. Chris hits on everybody. It doesn't mean a thing. Understand?"

"Thanks for telling me," I said with dignity, "but I had already figured that out."

He shrugged. "Well, all right then." He thrust his hands in his pockets and slouched off.

I could feel my mouth puckering as if I had bit on a lemon. At least now the suspense was over and I knew what P.J. was going to do to ruin Chris for me. I pulled the box of books inside my room and pushed it up against the wall. I wondered if it was too late for me to call Mindy's folks and beg them to give me a good home.

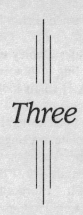

Three

The next morning when we drove off to school together, P.J. was cheerful. I guessed he must be looking forward to school, hard though that was for me to imagine. He was holding on to the steering wheel and had a slightly insane grin on his face that reminded me of someone. At first I couldn't think who. Then it came to me—Toad of Toad Hall. It was not school that P.J. was excited about but his new car.

"I got to pick up Dooley and Chris," he said. "I'm the first one of us to get a license, see?" The look of glee on his face was almost indecent.

P.J. drove up to a cedar-shingled house with a Jeep parked out front and leaned on the horn. "Dooley's dad travels a lot," he explained, "and sometimes old Dooley forgets to set the alarm."

"Can't somebody else wake him up? What about his mother?"

"Don't ask," warned P.J. "She's out of the picture. Totally."

After a few minutes Dooley came hopping out the front door holding a shoe in one hand. "I'm coming!" he yelled. His hair looked as if starlings were nesting in it.

I slid forward and he crawled into the back seat, the smell of chocolate wafting up to the front. Glancing behind me, I saw that he was eating a slightly squashed candy bar. "Breakfast," he explained, biting into it. "I forgot to set the alarm."

"Would you like to borrow my comb?" I asked.

"Comb? Oh, yeah, thanks." He ran his fingers carelessly through his ocher-colored hair.

P.J.'s Camaro tooled farther up the hill, and we stopped in a driveway next to a mailbox marked "Hamilton." Chris charged out at once. His eyes were the clear blue of an aviator surveying high altitudes. He was gorgeous, but I was able to avoid actually staring at him. Chris crawled into the back seat of the car. "Ready for school, campers?"

I cringed at the cheerful sound of his voice. All too obviously he was a morning person. In my humble opinion they should not be allowed to breed and reproduce.

P.J. stepped on the gas. "If I just don't get Killwein for English, I won't ask for anything else," he said. "If I get her, there's nothing for me to do but break both legs and get home tutoring."

"Forget it. That's no good," said Chris. "They'd

just get a wheelchair for you, and Andie'd have to drive you to school."

"Hey, Andie hasn't had driver's ed., man. She can't even get a learner's permit until Christmas."

The three boys observed thirty seconds of silence in sympathy. If I had had a nail handy, I could have bitten it through with my teeth.

The car plummeted down the road descending the knoll, and we then proceeded at an excessive speed through the streets of the town. Speed does not frighten me, but I'm not exactly crazy about it, either. In my view, if my father had stuck to a sane thirty-five miles per hour he would be alive today. I didn't say anything, of course. If I was going to have to live with P.J., I couldn't afford to preach to him. He was hard enough to get along with as it was.

Behind me in the back seat Chris suddenly growled. I jumped, held my hand over my quickly beating heart, and decided I was going to have to give up that extra cup of coffee in the morning.

"Jeez, don't you just love Andie's hair, guys?" All at once Chris was running his fingers through my hair. I shot P.J. an alarmed sideways glance.

"Cut it out, Chris," commanded P.J. "You want to walk or something?"

"Jeez, can't a guy just appreciate? What is this?"

I knew that when I wrote to Mindy and Lianne and told them I was carpooling with three boys, they'd be green with envy. Especially if I threw in the bit about Chris running his fingers through my hair. But the simple truth was that none of these guys was a realistic prospect for romance, and even if any of them had been, I wasn't sure I'd have been up to coping with it at eight in the morning. Dooley gave me my comb back, and I did my best to put my hair to rights.

"Look," P.J. said, "you give Andie a hard time, and my dad'll have my hide nailed to the garage door."

"Andie doesn't mind, do you?" asked Chris.

"Actually, I do," I said primly.

"See?" said P.J. "You heard me, man. Cool it. Got that straight?"

Strangled laughter from the back seat.

"Chris would short out if he tried to cool it," Dooley complained.

"What's that supposed to mean?" Chris yelped.

"Look, man," said Dooley. "We know you can't help it. It's like, well, a nervous tic or something."

P.J. cleared his throat ostentatiously. "Listen, guys, I've thought about this some and this is the word. Now listen—Andie's got to be like one of the gang. It's just too darn messy any other way, with us driving to school together every day and all. See what I mean?"

"You're going to have Andie thinking I'm a predator or something," Chris protested. "For pete's sake, cut it out."

"If the shoe fits—" muttered Dooley.

"This is it!" P.J. pulled up in front of the school. "Here we are, folks."

Architecturally my new school had everything— breezeways, detached buildings that abutted on dark woods, and two vast parking lots. I even spotted a cupola on the administration building.

This collection of brick buildings was scattered carelessly over a broad expanse of green lawn. Since I was used to a single building with roughly the layout of a high security prison, I thought the buildings didn't look like a school at all. A vast assortment of kids of great ethnic variety sprawled out on the lawn in small groups. A boy walked by us with a pierced ear, a pierced nose, and a thin gold chain connecting the two. No one seemed to notice him.

"I'm going to drop you off here, Andie, since you've got to sign up for your courses and everything."

"How do I find you after school?" I asked. I was getting a sudden insight into how Hansel and Gretel must have felt.

"Meet you in the east parking lot."

Great. The east parking lot reminded me of the one at Disneyworld except that the rows were marked Junior and Senior instead of Sleepy and Dopey. The only thing that kept me from breaking down was that I had resolved not to let P.J. see me cry.

"Don't forget to sign up for driver's ed.," P.J. said. A horn blared behind us. "Get out," P.J. urged. "I can't park here."

I got out and the Camaro sped off. So much for P.J. showing me around. I squared my shoulders and walked toward the administration building. "I like new challenges," I muttered. "I'm at my best under pressure." I didn't know why I was lying like that. Nobody was around to hear what I was saying except a troll-type boy with green spiked hair and matching eyebrows. He looked at me with alarm and moved on.

I have heard people say that the first day at a new school is always long. It was pretty clear to me this one was going to be no exception.

Later, in the hall after third period, I spotted Rachel Green's painter's hat bobbing along just ahead of me. I ran to catch up with her. "Hey, I've got to find B-two-eleven!" I cried. "Help!"

"Come with me," she said. "I'm on my way there myself."

I hugged my books to my chest and scurried along beside her. "This place is so big, so spread out," I panted. "I don't know how you do it. Seven minutes between classes and you get detention if you're late. I may not be able to cope with this."

"No problem," she said airily. "Like suppose you're not going to make it to B-two-eleven by the bell. Then you just go in the nearest class. Voilà! Technically, you're on time."

"But you'd still be in the wrong class."

"But the teacher in that class wants to get rid of you, right? So she writes you a hall pass. Then you just go along to your class at your own speed. You have to know how to work the system."

"I can see I have a lot to learn," I said humbly.

"A little applied intelligence can solve most problems." Rachel pushed her glasses up on her nose. "Now we go along the breezeway for a quarter of a mile or so. I am seriously considering roller skates. This used to be two schools until they combined them and linked them with this stupid breezeway, so the planning is not exactly logical. We've got two offices, two cafeterias, two parking lots, and no air-conditioning. Completely illogical, but cheap, which is all the school board cares about. The basic thing to remember is that the administration thinks they have everything under control, but it's all an illusion." She looked at me owlishly. "Also, do not let anybody lure you back to the Injun earring building."

"The what?" I asked nervously. Sometimes she talked so fast I wasn't sure I got it. Could there really be an Injun earring building?

Pointing out a window of the breezeway, she indicated an outbuilding near the woods. "The building where they teach draftsmanship and small engine repair," she explained. "The engineering building."

"I don't think I have to worry about being lured," I said nervously. "Nobody even knows me yet."

Benches were lined up along the breezeway, and a few of the more blasé kids were sitting on them, shuffling papers and eating candy bars. If I had tried to eat a candy bar and make it to my next class in seven minutes my stomach would have churned. But Chris obviously had a sturdier digestive system. He was sitting on a bench between identical blondes in identical letter sweaters. "Hi, Andie!" he yelled. He waved his candy bar at me.

I waved back and hurried to catch up with Rachel. She was climbing the stairs that were neatly labeled Up.

"I see you already know Chris," Rachel said.

"And since he knows everybody, it will probably be only a matter of time till you rise to the top of the social heap."

I wasn't sure that I bought this optimistic scenario, but I liked the sound of it. We had reached the second floor. A guy in boots stepped on my toe, and when I jumped out of his way I was clobbered by someone's book bag. My head was ringing as I faced the traffic jam at the door to my classroom.

"Chris is very popular," Rachel went on. "Have an animal cracker." Freeing a hand from her books, she somehow managed to hold out a crumpled package. "We're there. Here it is—B-two-eleven. American history."

I gulped down an animal cracker and filed into the class behind Rachel. I sank gratefully into a desk and tried as best I could to savor the ninety seconds of leisure before the bell.

When the bell rang, the teacher, Miss Wrigley, a petite young woman with frizzy blond hair, locked the door and began calling roll. Someone banged so hard on the door that it rattled. Miss Wrigley glanced in that direction, but obviously she had been carefully briefed about the tardiness policy, and she went on calling roll. Very possibly she was the only person in the room who was more nervous than I was. Her hands were shaking. "Elwood P. Joyner," she said. "Is Elwood P. Joyner here to-day?"

Some guys near me looked at one another and laughed. Finally one of them said, "If he was here, you'd see him."

Several people around him echoed this sentiment.

I wondered if Elwood P. Joyner had been the poor sucker pounding on the door. Right then he was probably reporting to the office to get a hall pass and to sign on for detention. I was just glad it hadn't happened to me.

I was having a bad enough time coping with this utterly misleading sensation that I knew where things were. I could feel the presence of the dry cleaners behind the school. I sensed the existence of a nearby alleyway that was a shortcut to the library, and a park bench near the bus stop where the sun always shone in the morning. These places were like latitude and longitude marks that fixed my location in the confusingly large universe. The only trouble was these landmarks were in my old hometown, not in Westmarket. The reason I kept feeling their presence was that my mind refused to admit that I was adrift in the galaxy, slipped from my moorings.

Lunch, after fourth period, was the worst. I came out of the lunch line holding my tray so tightly that my fingers went numb. When I looked around the room for someplace to sit, I spotted a place next to a couple of pink-cheeked girls in oversize shirts at the end of a large table. They didn't wear nose rings and their fingernails were clean. So far, so good. I approached them. "Hi," I said, smiling. When they looked up at me, their eyes were like bottle glass. Feeling uncomfortable and unsure what to do next, I sat down and opened my milk carton. The two of them rose at once and moved to another table. My ears burned. Suddenly I understood how the guy felt that was featured in the headlines reading "Deranged Postal Worker Kills Ten." Somebody probably got up and left him sitting alone at the lunch table.

"Greetings." Rachel slid into the seat beside me. I would have fallen on her neck with kisses if I hadn't preferred to remain as inconspicuous as possible.

"I see you met Finney and Angie," she said.

"I guess. Uh, I have the feeling I haven't quite risen to the top of the social heap yet."

"It's nothing personal." Rachel settled her thin frame into her chair, her glasses glittering beneath her painter's hat. "Those two think that sitting with anyone who's not in their clique will pollute them. All the people they go around with have this special way of talking and walking and acting, and if they ever deviated from it in the slightest, they would be socially dead. Like, there was this girl from that clique who dated a kind of redneck guy, and after that they all dropped her. They said she was starting to act like a redneck. I never did figure out what they meant by that because she seemed just the same to me." Rachel dug a fork into her mashed potatoes. "The nearest I could come to it was that they were talking about some sort of ritual uncleanliness like when the Brahmins accidentally brush up against the Untouchables in India. I been doing a lot of reading on the Untouchables lately. It's quite interesting. In fact, the entire traditional social structure of India has much to teach us about the social structure of the American high school."

P.J. rested his tray at the end of our table just then. "So, Andie, did you sign up for driver's ed. or what?"

"Next period."

"I got Killwein for English," he reported glumly. "Wouldn't you know it?"

I was glad to see P.J. Even him. It suddenly hit me that maybe he wasn't a bad sort after all. A little sour at times, maybe, but, hey, I wasn't always a ray of sunshine myself.

Right behind him were Chris and Dooley. I felt an overwhelming rush of warmth toward these guys who knew my name and would talk to me. Maybe they had got on my nerves in the car that morning, but that was before my morale had been beaten down by school. Now I was thrilled to see their familiar faces.

"Jeez, this place is a mob scene," said Chris.

Dooley promptly sat down and opened his milk carton. "Hey, how about let's just quit talking and sit down and eat, okay? I'm starved."

"You mean here?" asked P.J.

"Why not?" Chris sat down and promptly blew the paper wrapping off his straw. It landed on my head. I noticed Finney and Angie shooting me a vicious glance. They were jealous, I was happy to note.

"You guys know Rachel, don't you?" I asked. "She lives next door to P.J."

"Sure," said Chris. "Hi, Rache."

"Hi," Rachel mumbled. She bent to cut her meat loaf, her face hidden by the bill of her hat.

"What do you say I get my dad to send me to a

psychologist?" P.J. said suddenly. "And maybe he'll write me a note to get me out of Killwein's class."

"What's he going to say?" chortled Chris. "Please excuse P.J. from English, he's got a pathological fear of infinitives? Give it up, man. Resign yourself. You're dead meat."

"What about if he says I've got a personality conflict?" argued P.J. "You've heard of that, haven't you? It's worth a try. No, wait, I've got it. I've got a fear of heights. I have to be moved to a ground-floor classroom. Simple, classic. Killwein's class is second floor. What do you think?"

"What is this?" Dooley croaked. "You've flunked English before, haven't you? What's the big deal all of a sudden?"

"That was eighth grade, man, when I had crazy Miss Henbrow. Eighth grade doesn't count. This is different. This goes on your transcript for college. I'm telling you I can't take another crazy lady."

"Whoa! P.J.'s thinking about college already." Chris's blue eyes smiled at me, and only my strength of character kept me from melting all over the table. It was one thing to tell myself that Chris came on to everybody, but it was another to stay cool when he was giving me that industrial-strength look. I tried a little deep breathing so I wouldn't hyperventilate. As double insurance, I did the six tables backward in my mind.

"The only thing is," P.J. said gloomily, "my dad would never go along with getting me out of Killwein's dumb class."

A slender girl with long fingernails came over and trailed her hand along the end of our table. Her hair was in a single loose braid bound at the bottom with a scarf. The braid looked as if it had been put up during a hurricane, yet somehow I knew it was the height of cool. Only people who are excruciatingly sure of themselves can afford to look that disheveled. "You going to make it to my party, Chris?" she asked.

He put his arm around her slender hips and grinned up at her. "You better believe."

She smiled vaguely at us all. "Y'all come. It'll be fun." When Chris let go of her, she walked away slowly. I watched her push open the cafeteria door, wondering how long it would take me to feel that sure of myself at this school. Would it happen next year? Before I graduated? Never in my lifetime?

"Was that an invitation or what?" I asked.

"Sure." P.J. darted an uneasy look at me. "But it's probably not your kind of party, Andie. Hundreds of people and all. A big bash. It's the kind of party where nobody gets invitations. They just hear about it and go."

"Is that what you're going to do?"

He glanced at Chris. "Well, sure. But it's different for you. It's not like you'd know anybody there."

"I'm not going to rat on you at home, you know," I said. "You don't have to look so nervous. What exactly do you plan to do at this party, anyway?"

Chris clasped his hands behind his head and stretched slowly. "Hey, you know, kegs, girls dancing on tables, people getting thrown in the pool, and then about two A.M. somebody calls the police. We always leave before then, don't we, guys?"

"Why, I *love* that kind of party!" I exclaimed.

P.J. looked at me in alarm.

"Just kidding." I unfolded my napkin in my lap. "Actually, I have this feeling I'm going to have a lot of homework this weekend."

Rachel continued cutting her meat loaf and eating it. I shot her a curious look. It wasn't like her to be so quiet.

"Jeez, I love school." Chris slid down in his chair and sighed contentedly. "Summer was so dead. Now, man, it's lights, camera, action." He tapped on his plate with his fork and chanted softly, "Oh, come with me—to the sea—to the sea of love."

Dooley snickered. "He means to the engineering building."

"It doesn't scan, man. 'Come with me—to the engineering building.' It doesn't go."

Rachel's face was completely hidden by the bill of her hat. She might have been hiding. In fact, she undoubtedly *was* hiding. Why else would she keep staring down at her meat loaf? It's not as if it were scenic.

"Nuts," scowled P.J. "I don't see why I had to get Mrs. Killwein. What have I done to deserve her?"

"Poor you," chanted Chris, "poor, poor pitiful you."

Dooley grinned.

"Cut it out, you guys," said P.J. "It isn't funny."

"Maybe a computer virus will wipe out all your class assignments," I suggested.

P.J. brightened. "Hey, it's an idea. Where do I get one of these viruses?"

"I think you have to make them up yourself," I said. "It's some kind of sinister computer program."

"I knew there had to be a catch," he groaned. "I'm dead meat."

After lunch, when Rachel and I were walking to class, I asked her if she was okay. "You aren't running a fever or anything, are you?"

She sagged against a wall and pushed her hat up. I saw that her face was as pink as if she had just stepped out of a hot shower. "It's not that. It's Chris!"

Somehow I had been afraid that's what it was.

"He's gorgeous," she said, and sighed.

"He's poison," I told her.

"You're trying to scare me away from him." Her shoulders hunched in resentment.

"Okay, I am. I admit it. But it's for your own good. P.J. says he hits on everybody. You can see it for yourself! You go with a guy like that, and it's like hopping up on a smorgasbord table. He's only tasting."

"I do not care to discuss it further," she said stiffly. She pulled her hat low to hide her face.

"And if you're thinking I want Chris for myself, you're all wrong," I said. "I was born with a strong instinct for self-preservation, and I'm trying to save you from yourself."

Rachel escaped the calm voice of reason by ducking into her next class.

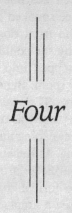

Four

I hadn't exactly intended to become best friends with Rachel. But the way those two girls, Finney and Angie, had treated me in the cafeteria made me realize it would be good to have an ally. Maybe Rachel was right. Maybe the two of us needed to watch each other's backs. Besides, I liked her. Nobody could call her boring. That afternoon I called her up and asked her if I could go over.

"You aren't going to try to talk me out of anything, are you?" she asked suspiciously.

"I just thought we'd go over our chemistry notes together."

"Okay, I guess you can come on over then."

I packed up all my books and went next door. I was looking forward to getting out of the house. Richard's place was so vast and so deeply carpeted, I couldn't even hear Mom's typewriter anymore, and since I had been hearing her typewriter my whole life, the silence spooked me.

Rachel opened the front door. *"Bonjour,"* she said. I didn't see why she couldn't just say hi like everybody else. I stepped into the foyer and followed her up to her room. Big surprise, her house was just like Richard's. They were not exactly alike, of course. Richard's place was rustic and rambling, while Rachel's was sweeping and swank. But they were both equally big. At Rachel's a winding stairway of pale green marble led from the entry hall to the upstairs. In the formal dining room off the entry hall, I could see a fireplace with a fern in it and tall Chinese vases. And, of course, the view was the same as Richard's with only an eight-degree difference in the angle. I just wished I knew where these people got all their money.

I had never been able to figure out why some people had money and others didn't. As far as I could tell, the people who had it were no smarter than anybody else, so I figured that it was some vast cosmic accident, like if you were standing in the right place, it just fell on you.

As far as I could see, the only thing Rachel's house lacked were tour guides, and with a place of that size they would have been convenient. The house had paintings with actual signatures, Oriental rugs, chandeliers, the works. The impressive interior decoration, however, stopped at Rachel's room, which was sort of like a slum in the middle of the Taj Mahal. I had to admire Rachel for putting her personal stamp on her space, but she had overdone it. When I followed her through her door, I actually had to pick my way through the debris. Clothes, books, papers, and sketches covered the floor. I suppose she noticed I was having a little trouble navigating.

"Mom says she doesn't pay Mary to pick up after me," she said. "And I like it this way because I know where everything is. Like my black turtleneck is under my bed and my chemistry notes are over here." She pounced on a bunch of papers near the dresser. "That's funny. I could have sworn they were right here." She frantically dived in the mess, rooting about. She flung papers up in every direction. "Honestly, I saw them just a minute ago." A handful of papers landed in the guinea pig cage near Rachel's bed. The guinea pig let out a squeal and scurried under its hay. I rescued the papers and laid them on the floor, but Rachel didn't even seem to have noticed the diversion.

It was then that I saw a huge chart taped to the wall over her narrow bed. I sat down on the bed and leaned toward it to get a closer look. "What's this thing you've got on the wall?"

She glanced up at me. "You might say that's my most ambitious study."

"Is it for some class at school or something?"

"Nope." She looked smug. "Actually, it's an in-depth study of Chris's girlfriends."

"What?" I did a quick double take. Now that I looked more closely I could see that the chart was covered with girls' names—Tracy, Susan, Tippy, Ingrid, Millicent, Amy R., Amy C. And that was only the beginning of the list. "Good grief!" I gasped. "He must have gone out with every girl in the school."

"Just about." She scrambled up. Skidding on an open magazine, she grabbed at the bedpost to steady herself. "I flatter myself that I have an unusually sound understanding of Chris's romantic history," she said proudly. "Of course, it doesn't matter so much *who* he goes out with. What I was really interested in was what made them break up. It was amazingly easy to gather data on that. People talk about Chris all the time at school, and you'd be surprised how often I was able to get a blow-by-blow account of the whole thing."

"Don't tell me. Let me guess—his trouble is girls keep catching him with someone else, right?"

"That did happen once or twice," she admitted. "But do you see the color-coded symbols?" She pointed to a black dot in the corner of one card. "This is where my analysis comes in. For example, the black dot shows the breakup was caused by gossip, like when some girl torpedoes the relationship by spreading a rumor. Okay, you can see right away that this would happen only if the girls are in Chris's group, because if you want to spread a rumor, you first have to be speaking to the people concerned, if you see what I mean. So girls outside Chris's social group don't have to worry about that particular problem."

"Unbelievable," I said. "I can't get over it. I mean, look at the number of girls we're talking about here! Talk about a cast of thousands!"

"Ah, but the thing you'll notice is that except for the card entries with the black dots, almost all these girls made some obvious mistake. Take Margie Sumner. When Chris first fell for her, he took her out to a fancy restaurant and then to a play in Durham. But he couldn't keep that up because he just has a Saturday job at the dry cleaners that doesn't pay all that much, so after that first big splurge they'd just split a pizza and watch a movie on the VCR. Margie started to whine and say he was taking her for granted."

"What a jerk."

"You've got it. When he said he couldn't afford to eat out every weekend, she said, 'Well, you could before.' So that was the end of her."

"Very stupid."

"She was a complete witch," Rachel said with satisfaction. "Hence the broomstick symbol on the lower right-hand corner of her card. Next came Jennifer Outlaw. Her problem was she was pathologically jealous. Every time Chris so much as touched another girl, she'd make a scene. One day she got into a fight with another girl in the school parking lot. They weren't actually throwing punches, but they were screaming and calling each other names, and Chris was so embarrassed he dropped her right then. You get the picture."

I certainly did. Chris was not exactly the perfect boyfriend for a pathologically jealous girl. I peered closely at the chart, noting that Jennifer had been annotated with a small emerald eye, presumably denoting jealousy. "But there are quite a few names here that don't have any symbol or note at all beside them."

"Well, naturally, I wasn't able to pin down what went wrong in absolutely every case. Sometimes he just went out with a girl once or twice and decided he didn't like her, I guess." She shrugged. "But I think I've got the main contours of his behavior."

"So, what did you learn from all this?" I inquired delicately. The lesson seemed so obvious to me. It wasn't as if Rachel could have any illusions left after her careful study. That wall chart practically screamed, "Keep your distance from this guy."

"Don't you see?" she cried, throwing her thin arms in the air. "I'm not going to make any mistakes!"

I blinked. "Run that by me again."

"You see, if Chris ever does notice me, if he ever asks me out, I'm going to be *ready*. I've done a careful study of it, and I won't make any of the mistakes that the others have made."

I started to ask what made her think Chris was going to notice her, but when I looked at the chart, the words died in my throat. The odds were with her. I had to admit it. Why would she be the only girl in the school that he didn't go out with?

Rachel paused a moment to straighten her hat. "And for my birthday," she went on happily, "I'm going to get contact lenses. I couldn't get them before now because my dumb sister Pamela was such a slob she gave up sterilizing hers every night and somehow she ended up in the hospital with an eye infection. So, then my parents said I couldn't have any until they were sure I was old enough to be really responsible. But now, you see, I'm not only responsible, I'm motivated. Extremely motivated." She swept her glasses off dramatically.

I had to peer closely at her to see her eyes on account of the painter's hat, but when I did I had to admit that she had fantastic eyes. They were large, almost violet, and fringed with black lashes that matched her long black hair.

"He's bound to notice me once I get contact lenses," she said.

It was a sad thing to see such a fine mind disintegrating under the influence of Chris's looks. With all the evidence right before her, Rachel couldn't seem to see that she was headed for disaster. She actually looked at that wall chart and saw it as a plan for true love!

"Why don't you ask for a car for your birthday, instead," I suggested. As a rule, I don't believe in telling people how to live their lives, but it was obvious that Rachel needed my help.

"I don't want a car," she said. "I want contact lenses."

"But if you had a car we could ride to school together. You'd be away from all those creeps on the school bus."

"If I got a car chances are I would just run it into a tree. With contact lenses I get Chris, and then I've really got something."

It was perfectly clear Rachel was incapable of listening to reason. She hadn't taken in any of my objections. She heaved a deep sigh, leaned her chin on her arm, and stared out the window. "There goes Chris now. See? I see him all the time going over to P.J.'s house."

When I followed her gaze, sure enough I saw Chris jogging on the street below. He was wearing an old T-shirt and jeans.

"So near and yet so far," said Rachel. "But one day he'll be mine. Just you wait."

She was a hopeless case. It was pretty clear that the only thing I was going to be able to do for Rachel was stand by and pick up the pieces. "So," I said. "Want to get down to chemistry?"

On my way back to the house I noticed that the garage door was open and thudding noises were coming from inside. Not that I'm a worrier or anything, but I naturally figured it was a burglar throwing all the household furniture downstairs while Mom typed away upstairs.

I peered inside very cautiously, but to my considerable relief it wasn't burglars at all but only Chris working out on P.J.'s bench.

Hearing my footsteps on the cement, he dropped the weights and sat up. "Hey, there. I was afraid to ring the doorbell since P.J. told us not to bother your mom when she's working."

"P.J.'s at the mall," I said. "He's looking for lacrosse shoes. Or maybe it's jogging shoes. I can't remember which."

"I thought he'd be back by now." Chris wiped the sweat off his brow with the corner of his T-shirt. His stomach had defined muscles that made it look rippled like a washboard. "Can I have something to drink, maybe?" He slid off the bench.

"I guess so." I went up to the kitchen with Chris trailing along behind me. I was hoping that Rachel didn't realize that I was entertaining Chris by myself. Not only would she have been jealous, but chances are she would have been over to borrow a cup of sugar in no time. I didn't want to have to stand by and watch her go all red and incoherent again. It was too painful.

When I opened the fridge, I saw that it was packed with food. Mom must have spent the morning grocery shopping. I handed Chris a cold drink, noting with some pleasure that being near him did nothing for me at all. Maybe it was Rachel's wall chart that did the trick, but at last, reason had triumphed over my hormones.

"Have you got anything that would go with this?" he asked. "Something to eat, maybe?" Not waiting for my answer he pulled a package of salami out of the fridge and then found a loaf of bread. He was obviously right at home in the kitchen. "Cheese?" he inquired hopefully. "Hold on, I think I see the mustard."

I got a glass of milk and a stick of celery for myself, then sat down and watched as he assembled a sandwich that contained enough calories to sustain an Indian village for a week. I wished Rachel could have seen him. His T-shirt was soaked with sweat and ringlets of hair clung to his forehead. He was grubby and he definitely smelled. Altogether he was far from the hunky vision he had appeared to be in the morning. However I was forced to admit he still looked good. My better judgment told me that probably Rachel would have needed stronger medicine than this to cure her addiction. When he put his feet up on a nearby kitchen chair and took a bite of his sandwich, his big toe popped out of a hole in his old sneaker.

"You know, Andie, it's really better like this, you being part of the gang."

"Oh, I agree." It was just possible I said it more enthusiastically than was really polite, but I wasn't worried about that since Chris was clearly not the sensitive type.

He gestured largely with his sandwich. "The thing is this, if you're like a civilian, you can really give me this insight into the way girls think. You follow me?"

"Sure, I follow you."

He sighed and tucked in the loose bits of his lettuce. "Great. Now, there's this girl—she's just fantastic, you know? Big eyes, soft voice, a little bit of a thing. There's just one problem. I don't think she speaks English. Her family runs this new Vietnamese restaurant in town, and I get the idea they haven't been in the country very long."

I knew the girl he meant. Suzanne Tran Van Kha. She was in my driver's ed. class. Since practically everybody else had taken driver's ed. in the ninth grade, ours was a very small class, made up exclusively of recent immigrants to the state.

"You might try saying hello to her," I suggested. "Also, and this is just a suggestion, don't grab her."

Chris shuddered. "Jeez, no. The thing is her

family might be really old-fashioned. I mean, I don't want to start a Tong war or anything."

"You're getting your countries mixed up. I don't think the Vietnamese have Tong wars."

"Besides it never crossed my mind to grab her. What kind of guy do you think I am, anyway?"

"I just noticed that you do tend to touch people a lot."

"That stuff with your hair really bothered you, huh? Look, I'm sorry about that. I guess I kind of get carried away. I mean, heck, you're an attractive girl."

This would have been somewhat more flattering if I had not just been looking at the list of girls Chris had previously found attractive. As it was, I was able to contain my enthusiasm.

"Anyway," he concluded, "I didn't realize you were such a shy type when I first met you."

"I'm *not* a shy type," I said. "I'm just trying to tell you you can't be too careful with this cross-culture stuff."

"Look, I hear what you're saying. I thought of all that. But, no kidding, Andie, give me your opinion. What about my problem? How can I get to know her?"

I sat down. "Tell me about it from the beginning. Where did you meet her?"

"She's in my French class. She and Madame Vanderwort were chattering away all over the place."

"So, talk to her in French. That's easy."

"Only thing is my French isn't that great. In fact, it stinks. I don't want her to laugh in my face."

45

I considered the way his blond hair tended to fall in soft petals, like those of a chrysanthemum. I also considered the bulge of muscle when he flexed his arm. Dispassionately, of course. Having my reason triumph over my senses did not keep me from appreciating Chris as a purely aesthetic phenomenon. "I don't know," I said finally. "But something tells me you'll find a way."

"It's just that I can't think of anything else since French class today. It's driving me crazy."

P.J. pushed open the kitchen door. "I didn't know you were here, Chris. Jeez, do you stink!"

Chris scratched his forearm and blew on it. "It must be these shoes. Anyway, I've been working out. I think you need to oil that NordicTrack or something, man. It's squeaking."

I picked up my milk. "See ya," I said. "I'm going to finish my homework."

"Look at Andie!" Chris sputtered.

I froze and checked myself over. To my relief nothing I was wearing had split.

"No, no," said Chris. "Keep on walking. Watch, P.J. Look, Andie, no offense, but you walk like a duck."

"I do not!"

Chris shrugged. "An armadillo? Funny, anyway."

"Don't listen to him, Andie. He says I walk like a duck too."

"What can I say, man? It must run in families."

"I don't think Andie walks like a duck at all." P.J. grinned. "More like a pigeon."

It wasn't easy to get out of the room, considering

how self-conscious I had gotten about my only means of locomotion. I had gotten as far as the stairs when I heard the phone ring.

"Andie, it's for you!" P.J. yelled. "Take it upstairs, will you?"

I ran upstairs and picked up the extension in my room.

"Andie? It's me, Rachel. I just saw P.J.'s car drive up. And Chris hasn't left yet, has he? I would have seen him if he had. That means you and Chris were alone in the house together," she panted. "Tell me what he said. Tell me what happened. Tell me everything."

"He said I walked like a duck."

"What?"

"That's what being a part of their gang means," I said tartly. "They tell me I walk like a duck. Honestly, Rachel, since I've moved down here, I'm getting more insight into the male mind than I really want to have. I don't need to be bitter and disillusioned at the tender age of fifteen."

"You aren't making any sense. Look, Andie, if you want Chris for yourself, just say so. I'm not afraid of competition."

"I *don't* want Chris for myself!" I exploded. "He just came over here to go in the garage and use P.J.'s gym equipment and to eat everything in sight. You don't have a thing to worry about."

"Wait a minute. Where are you?"

"I'm up in my bedroom."

"But wait a minute. It was P.J. who answered the phone. I recognized his voice."

"He and Chris are down in the kitchen."

47

"Eeek! There's an extension down there? What if they're listening?" A sudden click severed the connection.

I stared at the receiver in surprise. If Rachel thought Chris and P.J. were interested enough to pick up the phone and listen to our conversation, she was totally losing it. I shook my head. But then I already knew that, didn't I?

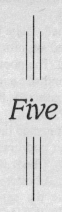

Five

The next day Elwood P. Joyner showed up in history class. I realized at once that he couldn't have been the kid who had been banging on the class door the day before because if this guy had banged on the door, it would have caved right in. He was that big. He wasn't fat and he wasn't musclebound, either. The adjective that sprang to mind was simply *big*. His dark hair was close-cropped, and there was the suggestion of a mustache on his upper lip. I found myself staring at him in fascination. His ears, his fingernails—everything except the freckles on the back of his neck was made on a large scale.

At least our teacher, Miss Wrigley, seemed to have gotten ahold of herself. There was color in her cheeks, and the grade book didn't shake as she called roll. She proceeded down the list with a reasonable degree of confidence. "Elwood P. Joyner," she said.

A deep voice boomed, "The name is Pete."

Miss Wrigley stared at him. "Y-yes, sir," she said, then blushed red. The poor woman had got so rattled that for a second she had forgotten she was the grown-up. I sympathized. Pete Joyner was big enough to throw anybody.

As soon as she had finished the roll, Miss Wrigley took refuge behind her podium, clutching it as if it were a life preserver. "Class, I want you to begin thinking about your semester projects. For your project you will have the experience of writing some history yourself, instead of just reading it. You are to choose some aspect of the history of Westmarket, do research, and write up a paper."

"Are you going to tell us what to do?" someone asked. He was wearing a T-shirt decorated with the Confederate flag.

"No," she said. "Certainly not. Part of the job is coming up with your own topic."

"But what if we don't know what to do?"

"Then you have to figure out what to do." Miss Wrigley was getting pink. "You might be interested, for example, to learn how the railroad came to Westmarket."

"I'm not."

"That's just an example."

"I'll do the railroad thing," said a fat boy.

"It should be something that interests you," said Miss Wrigley doggedly.

"Like what? You gotta give us some examples," someone whined.

"You have to think of them yourself," she said. Some alarming topics evidently came to her mind because she added quickly, "Of course, check them out with me, first. Now, I expect you to work with a partner on this project."

Rachel smiled hopefully in my direction.

"And I've already assigned the partners," Miss Wrigley went on.

My partner turned out to be Pete Joyner.

"Just don't let him fall on you," Rachel said to me when the bell rang. "What do you want to bet Miss Wrigley doesn't last till Christmas?"

Pete caught up with me after class. It took him longer to make his way through a crowd than most people since he needed more space to squeeze by. He touched my shoulder. "Andrea?"

"Everybody calls me Andie," I said promptly.

He winced. "I understand your problem." His voice was like a bassoon playing against the treble chatter around us in the hall. "They named me after my grandfather and not to complain or anything, but it's just about ruined my life. Look, I don't want to go putting this project thing off to the last minute. Let's get together pretty soon and decide what we're going to do. I like to be organized."

"Oh, me too," I said, eyeing him with fascination. He spoke the way he moved, rather slowly, as if he were afraid he might break something.

He pulled a pad out of his hip pocket and licked the tip of his pencil. "Thursday, October first, is okay with me, what about you?"

"Fine."

"You listed?"

"Well, my stepfather has a different name. I better give you my number." I shifted my books to one hip and wrote my number on his pad.

"We could meet at the library at three. You're not going to forget about this, are you? You need me to remind you?"

"I'll, uh, put it on my appointment calendar as soon as I get home." I didn't like to confess that I did not own an appointment calendar. There was something intimidating about Pete. I guess it was his size. His voice seemed friendly enough. "See ya," I said quickly. Then I took off.

The people at Westmarket High seemed to get to me more than the people at my old school. I wasn't sure whether it was just because I was on edge or what. Maybe subconsciously I expected everybody in Westmarket to be like Richard, the white bread sort of person. I had read about life in small-town America, I had seen Norman Rockwell calendars, and I guess I expected the school would be made up of bouncy cheerleaders and guys with freckles and good intentions. I didn't expect to see a guy with a nose chain. And that morning I had been startled when I passed a dark locker alcove and someone lurking in there had yelled, "The South will rise again!" Still less was I prepared for a giant like Pete Joyner.

I looked around for Rachel at lunch. When I didn't see her, I sat by myself, resolving in the future to bring a paperback book to school to read during these awkward moments. I wondered why I couldn't go to school and collect my grades the way adults go to work and collect a salary. Strictly business—that was the attitude I aimed for. I wanted to give up on the whole idea of being accepted at this more-than-weird school. I was sick of getting a burning pain in my stomach when I got to the cafeteria and didn't recognize anybody. I didn't know any of these people. Why did they have to matter so much to me? It wasn't sensible.

"Hi," said a male voice. "Anybody sitting here?"

"No, nobody at all." I smiled when I recognized Mike Evers, who was in my driver's ed. class. He was an army brat whose family had just been rotated back to the States after two years in Germany. He was so cute that it didn't even matter to me that he couldn't drive a car yet. I'd be happy with him on a bicycle built for two.

Mike pulled out a chair, but suddenly P.J., Dooley, and Chris swarmed the table. It was like locusts on the wheat field or fat cats at a fund raiser—suddenly they were all over the place. P.J. fell into a chair. "Look at this meat loaf," he groaned. "What do you think they put in it?"

"I don't even want to think about it," said Chris. He sat down beside me and put his arm around me. I looked at him in blank astonishment.

Mike Evers mumbled something about seeing a friend and disappeared.

Chris's arm dropped from my shoulder then, and he began seriously attacking his food.

"How are you getting along with Suzanne Tran Van Kha?" I asked acidly.

"Like a house on fire." He grinned.

I stared at him a moment in exasperation. "I wish you guys would show a little tact."

"Tact? What's that?" asked Chris.

"I think it's a low-calorie high-fiber cracker," said P.J. "My dad eats it for breakfast."

"No, no, I've got it." Chris leaned back in his chair so far that it tottered. "Tact—didn't he come in third in the Kentucky Derby? Yeah, I've got it, Tact, by Finesse out of Velvet Glove."

I narrowed my eyes. "You did it on purpose, you creeps."

P.J. gestured with his fork. "Andie, the guy was a dork."

"Perfectly obvious," agreed Chris.

"You don't even know him. He just got in the country a week or two ago."

"It looks like we stepped in just in time, P.J. She was actually getting to know this guy."

Dooley looked up. "I think this meat loaf is pretty good. Maybe they'd give me the recipe. What do you think?"

"Dooley does his own cooking," P.J. explained.

"That's why he's so skinny," said Chris. "Say, Dooley, don't you wish you had as many muscles as Andie here?" He squeezed my arm judiciously. I jerked it out of his grasp.

I saw Rachel then. She stood about five feet away holding herself rigid. Chris glanced idly in her direction. At that point her nerve gave out, and she turned and skittered away.

"We're not too popular today," Chris observed.

"You must be mistaken," I said. "How could anybody resist your famous charm?"

Chris grinned incorrigibly. "Actually, hardly anybody does."

"You're not going to tell Dad we've been giving you a hard time, are you, Andie?" P.J. gave me an anxious look. "I mean, we were just fooling around. Lay off her, Chris. She's getting mad."

"Who, me? Me, mad?"

Dooley prodded his meat loaf discontentedly. "The recipe probably wouldn't do me any good anyway," he said. "I mean, like it probably says stuff like 'Take six hundred pounds of hamburger.'"

I tried to imagine myself engaging Mike Evers in casual conversation after driver's ed. class the next day. I would say, "You know that guy who had his arm around me? I can't stand him." No, no, that didn't hit the right note. If I sounded hostile, that might put him off. "My stepbrother is such a nut," I would say in a cheerful voice. "And his friend Chris is the world's biggest tease. By the way, he's *not* my boyfriend." I slumped. No, it was impossible. There was no way I could casually dispel the impression he had gotten.

"You got a headache or something, Andie?" asked Dooley. "You don't look so good. I've got an aspirin if you need it."

Chris raised an eyebrow. "Hey, aren't you supposed to leave all medicine with the school nurse, man? What's this? Contraband aspirin?"

"I always carry some spares in my loafers."

Dooley extended his loafer-clad foot out beyond the table. I saw that the little slot where pennies were put bulged in odd places with aspirin-size bulges. He shook his head. "Only thing is when it rains, it all melts."

"Yech. Dooley, you are weird."

"Practical. I'm just practical, man."

"You are weird. You're wearing out your pockets with all that stuff you carry."

"You never know when you're gonna need a bottle opener."

"Yeah, but a needle and thread? A corkscrew? Band-Aids? A compass?"

"Hey, I haven't had a compass since fifth grade. That compass stuff is ancient history."

Finney and Angie passed by carrying their trays and shot me a malevolent glance. They were envying me again, I suppose. The irony! I rested my head on my hands and wondered if I was ever going to be able to develop a normal social life.

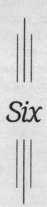

Six

"How do you spell that?" Rachel asked, her marker poised over an index card.

"S-u-z-a-"

"No, no, her last name."

"Oh, Tran Van Kha." I spelled it.

Rachel was making the latest addition to her wall chart. "I assume what broke them up was the language problem, right?" she asked. I could follow Rachel's thought processes very easily. She was thinking that language would certainly be no problem in her case. Just another impediment to the course of true love that she could safely strike off her list.

"I think the language problem was certainly part of it," I said. "Hang on. I took notes when Chris was telling me about it." I fished a crumpled piece

57

of paper from my pocket and tried to decipher my own writing, not an easy task. " 'She's a sweet girl,' and I'm quoting here, Rache, 'but we're just too different, ya know? Like I took her to a football game, and she kept covering her eyes and whimpering whenever anybody got tackled.' "

Rachel's eyes shifted. "I didn't know Chris was such a big football fan."

"He loves it. Never misses a game. He likes that thudding sound you get when one body socks into another and both guys land in the mud. He'd try out for the team if he could get his parents to sign the permission slip, but his father ruined his knees in a single semester of high school football, and now he won't let Chris play."

"Gee, Andie, you're the most fantastic resource. Not only do you see Chris all the time, but he keeps spilling out his guts to you. You're, like, his major confidante." She polished her glasses on the tail of her T-shirt and blinked at me anxiously. "That *is* all there is to it, isn't there?"

"Absolutely. I've explained to you a hundred times about my being their buddy and absolutely a civilian."

"Yeah, but you've heard about propinquity, haven't you?"

"Actually, no." I looked at her in alarm. "Is it illegal?"

"It's when you're around somebody all the time. That's propinquity. Studies show that it's an extremely important element in romance. I mean, statistically, people actually *do* marry the girl next door."

"But that would mean you and P.J.—" I was floored by the implications.

"I'm only speaking generally, of course. Statistics don't tell the whole story."

"Or worse, *me* and P.J." I swallowed. There was definitely something creepy about it. I don't suppose it would be incest technically, but it was just hard to imagine feeling romantic about somebody you saw at breakfast every morning—which had pretty dreadful implications for marriage when I stopped to think about it.

Rachel frowned. "The trouble is it's so hard to get any propinquity going these days. I guess people used to see more of their next-door neighbors than they do now. Maybe it's because of people having air-conditioning now instead of front porches. P.J., Chris, and Dooley all live right in this neighborhood, and I'll bet they don't even know I'm alive."

I happened to know this was true. I well remembered P.J.'s blank look when I told him I had met Rachel.

"I've got problems, too, you know," I said. "That boy in my driver's ed. class, Mike Evers, hasn't even looked at me since that time the guys scared him away from the lunch table."

"Oh, well," said Rachel, "there are lots of other starfish in the sea."

I looked at her in amazement. "I can't believe you said that."

She blushed. "All right, maybe I am just slightly fixated on one particular starfish. But it's different for you, Andie. You aren't in love. I mean, you aren't even in *like.*"

"I never will be, either, unless those guys give me some space. I swear, it's like having three permanent chaperons."

"I wish I had your problem. Having Chris around morning, noon, and night is something I could definitely get used to."

Personally, I doubted that she would like it as much as she thought. I couldn't seem to make her understand the difference between the way the guys were at home and the way they were in public. The difference was subtle, but it was there all right. When they were at school, they were cool, gallant, and macho. But when they were over at the house, they slurped milk directly from the carton, scratched themselves, and walked around on their hands. I wasn't absolutely sure I didn't like them better unvarnished, but it bugged me that Rachel thought their public images were their real images. I found myself constantly wanting to say, "Let me tell you something—" But it was hard to put what I thought into words without it sounding like sour grapes.

Rachel held the tip of her tongue between her teeth, concentrating intently as she taped the new entry onto her wall chart. "I think I could get used to football games if I tried," she said. "After all, football games are major cultural events in a way. I think it's time I found out more about football. Yes, sirree."

The funny thing was that on just about every other subject, Rachel was perfectly sane, even smart. It was just that when it came to Chris, her brain shut down.

She tossed some clothes off the bed to make space to sit. "I'm going to get my contact lenses day after tomorrow."

"I didn't realize your birthday was coming up so soon."

"Next week."

This could be important. "That means you'll be getting your driver's license," I pointed out.

"Yup. And my contact lenses, like I just said."

The girl had a one-track mind. "Yes, but when you've got your driver's license, your parents will let you borrow the car sometimes, won't they?"

"Sure."

"And we can go to the mall together and stuff."

Rachel shrugged. "I guess so."

I began to feel better. Maybe Rachel's driver's license wasn't important to her, but it was to me. It would give me a way to go places without my three-man escort. Not only was this desirable; it was essential. I didn't want the only boys in my life to be those who treated me like one of the gang. There had to be more for me to look forward to than that.

When I got home, Mom was in the kitchen with her feet propped up in a chair and a half-eaten apple in one hand. "How was school, sweet-heart?"

"Okay."

"Tell me about it. Have you met any nice kids yet?"

"Some."

"So you think you're going to find your niche here?"

"Absolutely. If I have to hack it out with a hatchet."

"You sound pretty grim."

"High school is no bed of roses, Mom."

"You don't have to tell me, sweetheart. I've been there, and believe me, once was enough."

I threw myself in a chair and contemplated my situation. At least it was not hopeless. Not completely. "The thing is there's this kind of caste system with the popular kids at the top and the nerds at the bottom. I don't have to be at the top. Coming in new I don't expect it. I just don't want to slip to the bottom."

My encounter that first day with Finney and Angie had left permanent scars. I was still having nightmares about not being able to find anybody to eat lunch with. And I was already dreading the winter flu season when Rachel might miss school and leave me totally dependent on the guys. Imagine having to beg them to sit with me!

"A lot of nice people are nerds, Andie."

"Oh, I know that." In fact, there were nerdish qualities to Rachel, though I was too loyal to dwell on them.

"Popularity doesn't prepare you for anything in this life. Some of the most popular kids I knew in high school didn't accomplish a thing afterward. They peaked at seventeen while the rest of us were just warming up. And the most out-of-it boy I knew became head of his own computer firm and came driving back to our tenth reunion in a Ferrari. How about that?" Mom looked at me triumphantly and took a bite out of her apple. "I sometimes think life should be subtitled 'The Revenge of the Nerds.'"

I managed to crack a smile, since I knew she expected it, but the fact was I was not entirely sure I had the strength of character to wait until I was twenty-six to be popular.

Mom tossed the apple core aside. "Do you see much of P.J. at school?"

"Sure. Besides the car pool, lots of times I eat lunch with the guys."

She smiled. "I told Richard he doesn't give P.J. enough credit. I think it's perfectly sweet the way he's taken you under his wing."

I didn't go into it because I was sure it would just get me another sermon on the unimportance of social success, but I was becoming more conscious every day that going around with the gang was a mixed blessing. On the one hand, they kept me from slipping down to the bottom of the social ladder—they did belong and I was all too aware that some of their glow rubbed off on me. On the other hand, they most definitely cramped my style.

Mom glanced at the clock. "I wonder where P.J. is. You don't think he could have forgotten this is Richard's birthday, do you?"

"Probably."

"Are you kidding me, Andie?"

"Well, nobody mentioned it to him this morning, and I think he's over at Dooley's. They were going to watch some horror flick on the VCR."

Mom jumped up in alarm. "I'd better call Dooley's house." A minute later she was frowning into the telephone receiver. "I'm just getting a busy signal. Do you know whether he got Richard a present?"

"Golly, Mom, how would I know?"

"I did remind him about it last week. Are you sure he hasn't mentioned it?" She redialed. "It's still busy. Andie, I think you'd better go over to Dooley's and get him. If you leave now, there'll still be time for him to go and get something for Richard."

"How am I going to get there?"

"Walk. You remember walk, don't you? It's what you used to do before P.J. started driving you everywhere."

"Okay, I'm going. I'm going."

"I'd better stay here in case Richard gets home early. I don't want him to find the house empty and wonder where everybody is."

I was glad I had already gone shopping and got Richard a suitably unobtrusive tie. Mom was giving off vibrations of panic that led me to believe Richard was one of those people who took his birthday seriously.

I tied my shoelaces and trotted up to Dooley's house. It was uphill all the way, and I was so winded when I got there that it was all I could do to manage a feeble knock with the door knocker.

"Come in," somebody called.

The first thing that struck me was that Dooley's house was ideal for watching a horror film. First of all, it was dark since all the blinds were pulled. And from what I could make out, it looked pretty bare.

There were no curtains, and instead of a carpet the living room had some sort of woven straw covering. The only light came in from the skylight in the kitchen, and that just spotlighted the piles of dirty pots and dishes.

When my eyes got used to the gloom in the living room, I made out the bodies draped over chairs and sofas, lit only by the flickering of the television screen. Considering the screams coming from the television set, all those inert figures looked sinister. I was only partly reassured by the strong scent of popcorn.

"P.J.?" I inquired timidly. No one heard me over the screams of the victims on screen. "P.J.," I said more loudly, "you've got to come home. It's your dad's birthday."

"Huh?" P.J. suddenly sat up straight. I jumped at the sudden movement.

"Turn it off!" yelped Chris. "We're going to miss the best part."

Dooley punched the panel on the VCR.

I pulled up a blind with a clatter. I was startled to see that white squares of cloth were pasted on the window panes. "Dooley," I said, "there are hand-kerchiefs glued to your windows."

"Don't touch those," Dooley warned. "They're drying. If I spread them on the window to dry like that, I don't have to iron them."

The guys were all blinking at me as if they were groundhogs coming up in February. I noticed the phone had been left off the hook, which explained the busy signals. My eyes were drawn past the phone and toward the open door of the kitchen. "I don't like to be nosy," I said, "but when's the last time you washed dishes?"

"I do them every Friday," Dooley said. "I have enough dishes to last me all week. Then on Friday I load the dishwasher and do them all at one time. It goes quicker that way."

"Is that, by any chance, a bicycle up there on your ceiling?"

"Yeah, neat, huh? People kept stealing my bikes, so now I just bring it inside. It's on a pulley with counterweights. I can get it down real easy." He reached to tug on a rope. After a moment's hesitation the bicycle sank to the ground. There it sat incongruously in front of the television.

"You should see the setup he's got at the bathroom window," Chris said. "He's got this sliding board that runs from the bathroom window to the garbage can, so he can just open the window and dump out the cat's litter box. The stuff goes right down the sliding board and into the garbage can so he doesn't even have to go outside. Dooley invented it himself."

I stepped over some socks and put the phone back on the hook. "Boy, Dooley, do you ever need a mother!"

Dooley flushed, picked up the bowl of popcorn, and carried it to the kitchen. He was obviously hurt. Now I was sorry I had said anything.

"His dad won't get in until Friday night, so he's got lots of time to clean up," Chris said.

"We were just getting to the good part of the

movie," P.J. complained. "What'd you have to come over here for?"

"Didn't you hear what I said? It's your dad's birthday. Have you gotten him a present?"

P.J. slapped his forehead. "Oh, my gosh, I thought his birthday was September thirtieth."

"This *is* September thirtieth."

"I gotta go, guys. I gotta go get some kind of present for my dad."

As we went out to the car, I spoke in a low voice. "Does Dooley live like that all the time?"

"Like what?"

"You know what," I said.

"I guess he is kind of casual. He's pretty much on his own, you know, until his dad gets home on the weekend. Don't be so picky, Andie. Live and let live is my motto. If you keep it up, you're going to start sounding like Dad. Why shouldn't Dooley have a good time? Why shouldn't he do things his own way? You've got to give people space."

P.J. dropped me off at the house and sped away.

Mom was wringing her hands in the kitchen. "Well," she asked. "Did P.J. remember?"

"Not exactly. But he's going to go buy a present right now."

"I'm home!" I heard Richard mounting the stairs from the garage. He threw the kitchen door open and stepped inside. "P.J. not home yet?"

"I guess he got held up," said Mom, glancing at me. "He ought to be here pretty soon, though."

Patience was not one of Richard's strong points. He glanced at his watch and began pacing the floor.

At last P.J. stepped in the kitchen door, a wrapped present held behind his back.

"About time," Richard grumbled. "You aren't going out to dinner like that, are you?"

P.J. gave a quick glance down at his sweatshirt and torn jeans. "Just give me a minute, okay? I'll change."

I could almost see the steam coming out of Richard's ears. Mom had certainly been right about Richard being hard on P.J. I mean, it wasn't as if P.J. had actually broken any laws. All he had to do was be fifteen minutes late and Richard would completely change color and start to have trouble breathing. It was weird.

"I guess I'll just go comb my hair or something," I said. If Richard was going to explode, I didn't want to be there to see it.

When I came downstairs again, Richard seemed to be in a better mood, though I noticed P.J. was eyeing his father with trepidation as we all got into the car. I never felt I really got a grasp of what was going on between the two of them. Taken individually they both seemed pretty okay. But together they made fireworks. Sometimes I wondered why P.J. didn't go stay with his mother, who lived in Germany with her second husband, a career military officer. I suppose he didn't want to leave all his friends. Also, there was the car. I guess he figured that the car made it worth putting up with the occasional storm at home.

We were going to go to a place called Davy Jones's Seafood Restaurant because Richard was a raw oyster freak. "I had lunch with Harvey Teller,"

Richard said on the way over, "and he told me about a heck of a thing. His boy got arrested for drunk driving last weekend. Can you believe that?"

My mom shook her head. "Awful."

"We're talking about a kid P.J.'s age. Trey is in your class, isn't he, P.J.?"

P.J. swallowed. "Uh, yes, sir."

"It seems he was at some wild party where the police got called, and the police stood up on a picnic table in the backyard and told everybody they had ten minutes to get out of there. Then as soon as Trey got in his car, they picked him up for drunk driving. Harvey was spouting off at me about how it was entrapment. Stupidest thing I ever heard, as if the police were pouring the stuff down Trey's throat and making him get in the car. I told Harvey right out that if I ever found out P.J. had been to a party like that, I'd yank his license so fast his head would spin. He could forget about having a car again—ever."

P.J. shot me an anxious look. I wondered if he'd been at the party where Trey got collared. For my part, I just felt very glad that huge, wild parties were not the sort of thing I lived for, because when Richard started going on like that in his ruler-of-the-universe fashion, it was very comforting to have a clear conscience.

When we drove up to the restaurant, we saw a sign that said, "Over fifty-five? Ask about our seniors discount card."

Richard groaned. "Look at that, El. It won't be long until I'll be eligible."

"Years and years," said Mom soothingly. "Why, you're in the prime of life, darling."

Richard checked himself in the rearview mirror. "I look a hundred. All that gray!"

"It's just the way the light is hitting it," Mom cooed.

"I've heard about this kind of thing your barber can do. It's kind of like reverse streaking. They don't dye the whole head. Just every other hair."

Mom gave him a gentle shove. "Shut up. You look terrific. Very distinguished."

Actually, Richard did look good for a man his age, but when I put myself in his position, I could see that having your hair turn gray would take some getting used to, no matter how distinguished it looked.

When we got inside, Richard went off to the men's room. "This is the first birthday you've had to share your dad, P.J." Mom tilted her head toward him. "I hope you don't mind."

"Nope," said P.J. "Actually, having you two around kind of helps. I don't know if you've noticed, but he's always getting on my case."

Mom reached across the table and patted his hand. "I think you two are just too much alike."

P.J. blanched a little at that, but didn't actually argue with her.

When Richard came back, he was in a better mood. "Ran into Ben Hicks." He leaned back and unfolded his napkin. "You should have seen him, Ellen, he looked horrible, poor old guy. I can't believe the way he's let himself go."

Mom smiled fondly. "Maybe while we wait for

our food, we can open some of your presents." She fished wrapped boxes out of a canvas bag. "This is from Andie. No, I'm wrong. This is P.J.'s. Why don't you open the kids' presents first."

The first clue I had that anything was the matter was when I realized both our packages were done up with the same wrapping paper. I gave P.J. an apprehensive look. Had he also taken advantage of Belk's policy of free gift wrapping?

Richard was still full of good humor as he ripped into P.J.'s present. "I can really use this," he said, surveying the gray pin-striped tie. "Just the thing for a navy suit."

"And funerals," put in P.J.

Richard smiled. "I don't want to talk about funerals just yet, son, if you don't mind. I hope the time hasn't come yet that my friends are dropping like flies." He opened my package next, and there it was, the identical gray pin-striped tie. I had a momentary impulse to climb under the table.

Richard put the two tie boxes next to each other and looked at them dolefully. "I wonder if you two are trying to tell me something."

"Great minds work in the same way," said Mom cheerfully.

It was just a good thing that Mom's present wasn't a pin-striped tie. She gave him a picture of herself in a silver frame. "That's for your office, to let the 'girls' know you're taken," she said.

Richard seemed to really like the picture. P.J. and I exchanged relieved glances. I suppose it was true, what Mom had said once, that bit by bit we would start to feel like a family.

Seven

Rachel flung the door open to greet me with a broad grin. "What do you think of them?"

"Of what?"

"Of my contact lenses, stupid."

I peered under the bill of her hat. Sure enough, I could make out her eyes. The familiar glint of the glasses was gone. "Very nice."

"Now I want to try them out."

"Like how? I thought we were going to work. I haven't even started studying for that unit test."

"You can do that anytime. Is Chris over at your house now?"

"I guess so."

"I saw him drive up with P.J., but I don't have a clear view of the other side of the house, so I wasn't sure but what he might have left already."

"Rache, if you quit watching the house, think of

73

what you could do with that time—learn a foreign language, become aerobically fit—"

She frowned. "Quit bugging me, Andie. Lead me to Chris. I want to try out some of that propinquity stuff."

"Why don't you just plug yourself into a wall socket? You'll get the same effect."

"I don't know what you're talking about."

"You know how you freak out every time you get around Chris."

"That was before I had contacts. Now I have newfound self-confidence. I'll sail into their midst with absolute preternatural poise."

"Maybe I'll wait here until you're done."

"I can't go over by myself!"

"I don't see why not."

"Because I can't, that's why. They'd wonder what I was doing over there. You've got to go with me."

Reluctantly I allowed myself to be dragged back to my house.

P.J. looked up in surprise when I walked in. He and Chris were in the middle of a six-course after-school snack. "I thought you were going over to Rachel's to study," he said, a trifle pointedly.

"We decided to study here," I said. Rachel poked me. "But first," I added, "we thought we'd get something to eat."

P.J. grunted.

I opened the refrigerator and stared at it helplessly. With all the tension in the air, the whole idea of food was repugnant. Not that P.J. and Chris were tense. They were draped over the kitchen chairs like cooked spaghetti. But Rachel and I had enough tension bottled up for all of us. "Want some ice cream, Rachel?" I asked.

"Thank you, that would be lovely."

I looked around at her, startled. Somehow Rachel had come out with golden, pear-shaped tones nothing like her usual tumbling, helter-skelter syllables. "Uh, you like ch-chocolate syrup on it?" I asked, badly rattled.

She lowered herself into a chair and waved a hand in a regal gesture. "Everything."

I took out syrup, maraschino cherries, nuts in syrup, whipped cream, everything I could think of that could conceivably go on ice cream. Then I went to the pantry and got out four different kinds of fancy sprinkles. I hesitated. "You want bananas, too?" I asked.

"You forgot the kitchen sink," said P.J.

I glared at him. Rachel and I sat at the counter adding junk to our ice cream until it started to look more ornate than edible. Not that we cared. Neither of us was hungry, and neither of us could think of anything to say. We were just waiting for some of that propinquity to go into action.

P.J. and Chris were talking in low voices. And since we were only ladling cherries and nuts and sprinkles, I could make out some of what they were saying, particularly during the moments that the refrigerator motor stopped humming.

"I thought he liked Jennifer Outlaw," said Chris.

"Nah, man. In fact, he's . . . mumble-mumble."

"No, kidding. Mumble-mumble."

"Don't believe it, man."

Laughter.

"Well, that's what I'm saying," crowed Chris. "What'd I tell you?"

While I was puzzling over what they were talking about, the refrigerator motor seemed to stop completely. Into the dead silence, P.J. said, "Are you going to eat that ice cream, Andie? Or just watch it melt?"

"We're going to have it bronzed," I said. I picked up my bowl of ice cream, lifted my chin, and marched to the stairs. Rachel reluctantly followed me, casting wistful glances over her shoulder.

Once we closed the door to my room behind us, Rachel flung herself on the bed and pounded the mattress with her fist. "He didn't even notice me!" she cried.

I eyed the door uneasily, hoping that P.J. and Chris hadn't decided to come upstairs. But when I reflected, I knew they wouldn't separate themselves from the refrigerator except in a dire emergency.

"He didn't even notice that I wasn't wearing my glasses," moaned Rachel.

"Come on, Rachel. It's not the end of the world. Life goes on."

Rachel wiped her nose on my candlewick bedspread. "Of course, this is just the first time he's seen me without my glasses, but I thought he would at least *notice* me. He looked right through me. This is so unspeakably embarrassing! How can I go back down there? How can I get out of here without him seeing me? This is awful!"

"You don't have to leave right now," I said. "We could study."

She stared at me in amazement. "You must be kidding. I can't study when something as important as this is going on."

The phone rang and I picked it up. A deep voice rumbled, "Andie?"

"Hello?" The line sounded suddenly hollow, and I knew P.J. had picked up the extension downstairs.

"It's for me," I told him.

"Andie, you there?" repeated the deep voice.

"Pete!" I gulped, suddenly recognizing the voice. "I forgot about our meeting yesterday."

"I thought you said you were going to put it in your appointment calendar."

"Yes, but, uh, the dog ate it."

"The dog ate your appointment calendar?"

"We've got to feed him better."

"Look, I don't want to go to the library and hang around for another hour unless I'm sure you're going to be there."

"I'll be there next time. I promise. When?"

He sighed. "Let's meet at my house. That way if you don't show up, at least I won't be killing the whole afternoon."

"Oh, I'll be there the next time. I won't forget."

"You'd better not. It's seven-oh-seven Gloucester Road."

"I'm writing it down." I wrote his address in the margin of my chemistry notes. "When did you say?"

"Two weeks from yesterday. Same time. I'm tied up next Thursday. Okay?"

"Okay."

"I'm going to remind you in history class."

"Look, I'm really, really sorry."

"Just make it next time."

"Oh, I will."

I hung up.

"Who was that?" asked Rachel. "Your friendly neighborhood loan shark?"

"This guy in history class that I'm supposed to be working on a project with. You know, Pete Joyner."

"Oh, wow. No wonder you sounded nervous. That guy could pulverize you with his little finger."

"I'm not nervous. I'm just embarrassed. I was supposed to meet him to work on that stupid history project and I forgot." I was so relieved to hear Rachel sounding more like her old self that I immediately forgot all about Pete Joyner. "So, what do you want to do? You want to study chemistry? Or I could tie some sheets together and let you out the window if you want."

"That won't be necessary," she said. "I can just go out the front door, and he probably won't even notice me."

"Right."

Rachel pounded the bed with her hand. "But he's *supposed* to notice me."

"But not now when your eyes are all red."

"Are they really that red?" She jumped up and peered at herself anxiously in my mirror.

"Well, maybe just a little pink."

"I wish I were dead."

I thought about saying a few words about how ill-suited Chris was to be the object of such a grand passion, but something told me this was not the right time. I walked Rachel downstairs and let her out the front door. As she had predicted, P.J. and Chris didn't even notice. They were in the kitchen stuffing themselves, and it would take more than the opening of the front door to distract them.

As soon as the door closed behind Rachel, the phone in the kitchen rang. By the time I got to the kitchen, P.J. was speaking into the receiver, but I couldn't hear what he was saying. "I'm going to take this upstairs, Andie," he said. "Hang it up for me, will you?"

As soon as P.J. left, Chris grabbed at the phone. "Haven't you heard of the right to privacy?" I hissed. I snatched the receiver away from him. As soon as I heard P.J.'s voice on the phone, I hung up.

"Who was it?" Chris asked.

"How should I know?"

"Did she have sort of a squeaky little girl voice?"

"Honestly, Chris. Even if I knew, it's none of your business."

"I'll bet it was Susie Skinner."

"Doesn't your own life keep you busy enough without you worrying about P.J.?"

"I'm between girls," Chris reported sorrowfully. I snorted.

Chris poured himself some more milk, then frowned. "Why do people have to get so possessive? You saw the way he was, Andie. What does he think? That I'm going to try to steal his girl or something?"

Probably, I thought. It had only just occurred to

79

me that having Chris as a best friend would definitely have its disadvantages. "You know what, Chris? You should get a hobby."

"What are you talking about? I do all kinds of things. Jeez, there aren't enough hours in the day." The milk had given him a white mustache, and he wiped his mouth carelessly with his sleeve.

"It just seems like you think about girls an awful lot."

"And I guess you don't think about boys a lot?"

"No, I don't."

"Liar."

"As if I had any boys to think about," I said indignantly. "Look at the way you guys scared off Mike Evers."

"Who?"

"That guy who was going to sit next to me at lunch."

"Oh, the dork. Never going to let us forget it, are you? Look at it this way, Andie. What kind of guy gets scared off when we come and sit down at your table? We were doing you a favor."

"Don't do me any more favors, okay?"

"Look, go out with any dork you want. See if we care."

"Thank you, I will."

"It's just that we're naturally going to take an interest. I mean, think about it. If you hook up with some creep and he starts hanging around over here, it'd be a pain for us, wouldn't it?"

I knew that it was hopeless to reason with the guys. They weren't capable of understanding my point of view. They seemed to think I should be perfectly content to tag along with them forever. My romantic strategy would have to depend on outwitting them. Fortunately, I didn't think this would be difficult.

Chris squirmed restlessly. "Jeez, P.J.'s talking to that girl long enough, isn't he?"

"Gee, I'm really sorry that you're stuck here talking to me."

"Cut it out, Andie. You going to give me a hard time?"

"Sure, I am. Why should things be any different now? Where's Dooley?"

"Friday afternoon he's always cleaning house. I promised to go over there in a minute and help with the dishes."

"Tell me the truth, Chris, don't you think Dooley's dad sort of neglects him?"

"Huh! I wish I had his problems. He gets to do anything he wants, whenever he wants. No mom nagging him to pick up his socks, no dad asking him all the time what he's going to do with his life. He's got it made."

"You don't really think that, do you?"

"I'm not saying I could live like that. I'd miss my folks. I mean, they drive me crazy, sure, but I'm kind of used to them. The point is, it suits Dooley. He's kind of a free spirit."

More like an orphan, I thought. "Whatever happened to his mom?"

"I think she went off and joined some cult when Dooley was little. My mom said she never even wrote or asked to see Dooley or anything. She just dropped out of sight. I guess she's in some airport somewhere handing out flowers and saying Hare Krishna in a spacy little voice."

"That's awful!"

"It is pretty bad, but if she was as weird as that, he's probably better off without her. Do you know Jeff Harlow?"

"I hardly know anybody but you guys, you know that," I said with some bitterness. "What's with Jeff Harlow?"

"It's just that his mother is weird and he's stuck with her, that's all. One minute she's all sweetsie in this phony kind of way, and the next minute she's screaming at everybody. She drinks. Dooley's got an easier time of it than old Jeff, I can tell you. At least Dooley can bring his friends home and not worry about his mom throwing a pot of chili in their faces." He shuddered. "Of course, it's going to be even better for Dooley when he gets his license. Do you know I'll be the last one, the *very* last one of us to get my license? I would have to have a November birthday." He sighed heavily.

Of course, Chris wouldn't be precisely the last one in the gang to get a driver's license. I would. The thought cast me into deep gloom.

Chris twisted around in his chair to check the door that led to the stairs. "What can they be talking about all this time?"

"I don't see why the idea of P.J. having a girlfriend bothers you so much. You've got girlfriends all over the place."

"That's different. With me it's not anything serious."

"Very true."

"What do you mean by that?"

"I was just agreeing with you."

"Cut it out, Andie. I caught your tone of voice. 'Very true,' you say in that funny voice like you're *thinking* something else. All I meant is how serious can anything get when I don't even have my license? Everywhere I go, I've got to have my parents drive me unless I get a ride with P.J. I might as well be in second grade." He cast another uneasy glance over his shoulder.

"You couldn't be jealous, could you?" I folded my arms and smiled at him. "I'll bet you're worried that P.J. is going to settle down with one girl and they'll spend all their time going off together by themselves and you'll be left out in the cold without a ride."

He smiled. "Not hardly, Andie. I may have my problems, but it's not like I have a big problem with being alone."

It struck me then with a sickening thud that if P.J. got paired off and started going off all the time with one girl, *I* was the one who was going to be left without transportation. Dooley would be getting his driver's license any minute, and Chris would be getting his in November. I was the one who was completely dependent on P.J. for transportation.

Chris caught my eye. "Who's worried now?"

I laughed a little. "Okay," I said. "I give in. I sort of wonder who he's talking to, myself."

"Probably Susie Skinner. You should have seen the way she was looking at him during algebra."

"What's she like?" I asked. "Is she nice?"

"She giggles a lot. She has a tiny little nose that

83

you'd hardly think anybody could breathe through. It's not like a nose at all, more like her face got pinched into a little point there. And she makes these stupid jokes, and she's always with a bunch of giggling girls. Yuck."

After a while P.J. strolled back into the kitchen with a look of elaborate unconcern.

"How's Susie getting along?" Chris asked.

"Huh?"

"Susie," Chris repeated patiently, "how's she getting along?"

"Okay." P.J. poured himself a glass of orange juice and gulped it down.

Chris and I looked at each other. I wondered how I was going to like going around with a girl who giggled and made stupid jokes. Not that I would necessarily get the chance to find out. If P.J. got serious about some girl, it was going to be the acid test of how much the car was truly "ours." I was afraid I already knew the answer to that one.

Eight

After I thought about it, I realized that P.J.'s interest in Susie Skinner was just one more reason for me to find myself a boyfriend. A girl can get along without a boyfriend easily, but it's pretty hard to get along without a car. What I needed was a guy with a valid operator's license. That let out everybody in my driver's ed. class, which was, unfortunately, the only class where I usually had a chance to talk to people.

I found myself checking out the boys in my other classes. Ideally, my prospective boyfriend should be someone I was actually attracted to, but I could feel myself getting less particular about that daily.

In French class, third period, I was watching a guy in the front row. His dark hair curled up a little just above his collar in a way that was charming. However, his lower lip sort of pouted out, and I was having trouble deciding whether he looked vulnerable or just petulant. While I was debating this weighty issue, my elbow knocked my pencil off my desk. The boy behind me picked it up and handed it to me. He didn't say anything, but he smiled in a friendly way. After a decent interval I sneaked a second look at him. He wasn't bad. In fact, I liked him better than the guy with the pouty lip. The bell rang and I shuffled my papers. I was hoping the boy who had picked up my pencil would stop and talk to me on his way out. He seemed to be in no hurry. He stood up and rested one knee on his chair seat.

"Gonna be at the mall tonight?" a guy in a bomber jacket asked him.

"Yeah. I guess so. What about you?" The boy I had targeted was now leisurely assembling his books. I noticed he had brown eyes. He was a couple of inches taller than me and dressed quite conservatively, as if he might be president of the Young Republicans Club.

"Sure, I'll be there. Nothing else to do," said the bomber jacket. "Tracy and me broke up."

"No joke. Sorry about that."

"Hey, no, it's cool, man. It's like being out of jail." The bomber jacket gave a short laugh.

I wondered if those two were ever going to quit talking. I thought boys were supposed to be so taciturn. Whatever happened to the strong silent type? They were behaving like old ladies at church.

I glanced at my watch, beginning to feel panic. People were clearing out. In a minute I would start to be conspicuous. Also, even more important, if I wasn't careful I was going to be late for history class. My pencil slipped out of my anxious fingers and bounced on the asphalt tile.

"Whoa." The boy with the brown eyes bent to pick it up. "Hey, butterfingers!" He handed it to me and our eyes met.

I stopped breathing. "Thank you," I gasped. Suddenly flustered, I grabbed my books and dashed out of the class, which wasn't what I had planned at all. A glance at the almost empty hall did nothing to calm my nerves. According to my watch, I had precisely two and a half minutes to make it to history. I took a deep breath, then broke into a run. Pausing on the stairs, I checked my watch again. I was never going to make it. My skin prickled at the thought of detention, and I started running again. As I reached the top of the stairs, the bell suddenly split the air with an electronic jangle, and I jumped just about out of my skin. I grabbed at the nearest doorknob, and almost before I knew it I had shot inside the classroom.

I smiled uneasily at the rows of kids staring at me. Beside the door was a surprised-looking teacher with iron-gray hair.

"Ooops," I said as I heard her click the door shut behind me. "I guess I got turned around. I thought this was my history class."

Chris happened to be sitting in the front row. He winked at me.

"Hold on," the teacher said. "Let me write you a hall pass." Something told me I was not the first to try this ploy with her. The lady had an air of world-weary disillusionment, and I knew she didn't believe my story about getting lost. But she scribbled out a hall pass and unlocked the class-room door to let me out.

I stepped out into the hallway and beamed at the official hall pass in my hands. Not only had I made contact with a genuine boy, I was actually working the system. I might just make it in my new school after all.

That evening I got to work on persuading Rachel to give me a ride to the mall. I had distinctly heard brown eyes say he was going there. Since I had blown my chance to talk to him after class, maybe there was still time to recoup the loss. All I had to do was casually run into him at the mall.

"But I was going to wash my hair tonight," Rachel protested. "And I don't want to go to the mall. I've never been very good at hanging out. I just don't have the knack."

"Take along a good book," I snapped. "Honestly, Rachel, I'd do it for you. All I need is a ride, not a kidney transplant. Don't you want me to have a chance to fall in love, just the way you have? Just go to the mall with me, give it an hour, and when we get back I'll braid your hair in cornrows." This was a rash promise because Rachel had a lot of hair, but I was that desperate.

"Really? Cornrows?"

"Absolutely. I promise."

"Okay, it's a deal."

I was really excited as we drove to the mall. I kept sort of jiggling up and down on the seat in Rachel's mom's Volvo. All kinds of uncharted possibilities lay before me. That guy in class had picked up my pencil twice, *and* he had smiled at me. That had to mean something. If it turned out that it didn't mean anything—well, I was flexible. There'd be other guys at the mall. The point is I was making a start. I was actually getting away from the guys. That was the main thing.

The mall was brightly lit and spilled radiance into the parking lot all around it. Rachel parked and we went in the main entrance.

"Where do people do this hanging-out?" she asked. "This place is so huge. Maybe we could just sit on the edge of a planter somewhere and read."

"I don't think so. I think we'll have to keep moving if I expect to have any chance of running into this guy." I checked the mall directory. "Okay, here's the way I see it. We'll start at the three-screen cinema, and then we'll go by the game arcade, then proceeding very slowly we'll go past all the places where you can get something to eat—pretzels, pizza, ice cream, whatever." One thing I had learned by living with P.J. was that boys are very seldom separated from food. "We'll just keep moving, and if brown eyes is here we're sure to see him."

Rachel looked at me curiously. She was not quite used to her contact lenses yet, and her eyes seemed unnaturally wide under her painter's hat. "What then?" she inquired.

"I don't *know* what then. I haven't ever done this before. We'll have to improvise, okay?"

First we went to the movie theater. The feature hadn't started yet, so quite a few kids were standing around outside. They were in groups of four and five in their expensive clothes and well-adjusted smiles. The way they stood seemed to say, "We were born here. We know everybody. We belong." I hated them at once.

"Do you see him?" Rachel asked, scanning the crowd.

"No, and I want to get out of here."

"I thought we were supposed to sort of cruise slowly." She had to run to catch up with me.

"Well, yeah, but let's not just stand. Let's at least move." I wanted to get away from the self-assured types standing in front of the movie theater.

We bought ice-cream cones and continued on our planned route. The lights of the game arcade blinked to our right, just past a stand of big-leaved plants that looked like holdovers from the age of dinosaurs.

I grabbed Rachel's arm. "Wait a minute, slow down. I think I see him."

"The guy in the bomber jacket?"

"No, no, the other one."

Rachel and I scooted closer to the arcade and pretended to study a window display of diamond sprays in the jewelry store next door. One was marked $3,872. I wondered if that included sales tax.

"What do we do next?" whispered Rachel.

"I don't know." I looked down at my ice cream. It was dripping on my sneaker. It's a terrible disadvantage to lose your appetite under stress. I have known people who only got through major traumas by eating Häagen-Dazs ice cream. Whenever my friend Lianne failed a test, she would curl up in bed under her down comforter and very slowly eat a pint with a teaspoon. After that, she would be ready to dust herself off and try again. Not me. When life is black I can't think about food. All I can think about is how black life is.

"Hullo! It's Butterfingers!"

My head snapped around. The guy with the brown eyes was standing so extremely close to me that I had to take a step away so that I would not risk dripping my ice cream on him.

"Ready for that French test?" he asked.

I returned his smile. "Sure. You can see how I'm studying, can't you?"

"Uh, your ice cream seems to be melting."

I looked down at it with dismay.

"Here, I'll ditch it for you." He gingerly took the sticky cone between his thumb and forefinger and walked over to a nearby trash container.

I was impressed. I thought he looked even better now than earlier. Rachel watched with bug-eyed fascination as he dropped the cone in the trash. "Is this what's supposed to happen?" she asked me.

"How do I know?" I whispered. "I'm new at this."

The boy came back wiping his fingers with his handkerchief. Somehow he managed to look neat and freshly pressed even in jeans.

"Thank you," I said. "I guess I just wasn't really hungry. Are you, uh, awfully good in French?"

"No, not awfully good, just awful." He smiled. "I'm really dreading this year. My sister had Robertson a couple of years ago, and she said it was the hardest course she ever took."

"That sounds pretty bad."

"I'm Jim Hedrick. I'm sorry, I can't remember your name."

"Andie Baker. And this is my friend Rachel."

"Andie!"

I looked around in confusion. Suddenly P.J. and the gang were upon us. I was surrounded. I could actually feel P.J.'s breath hot on my neck. "Jeez, I wondered where you were," he whooped. "I looked around one minute and you were gone."

Chris put one arm around me and the other around Rachel. "Where did my girl go, huh?" he cried. "Trying to get away."

Jim Hedrick looked confused. "Are you guys together?"

"No," I said promptly, but my voice was drowned out by P.J. saying loudly, "I'm Andie's brother." He was standing behind me poking me between the shoulder blades with his finger. "Have to keep an eye on her," he said. "You'd be surprised at the scum that cruises the mall."

"Terrible," agreed Chris, giving me a warm squeeze.

"Wait a minute!" I protested. I shook off Chris and wheeled around to face P.J. "Look here, this is beyond funny, you guys."

"I told them that," said Dooley, smiling foolishly. "I told them you were gonna be mad."

I turned to explain to Jim that my stepbrother and his friends were idiots, but he had vanished. He had melted without a trace into the game arcade, the spineless idiot. Blinking lights showed in the gloom of the arcade, and I could make out the occasional jacket or bright-colored T-shirt, but I didn't see any sign of Jim. And what would I have done if I had been able to see him? Lassoed him?

Chris wiped his hand against his pants. "You're sticky, Andie. You need to take a bath or something. Jeez, what a close call that was! Did you know Hedrick is the president of the Young Republicans Club?"

"I like young Republicans." I stomped my foot. "Oooooo!" I would have said something even nastier, but I was so mad I couldn't think straight. All that planning, all that work gone to waste.

"Something wrong?" inquired P.J. solicitously.

"Why don't we get something to eat," said Dooley. "I'm starved."

"You said it," Chris agreed heartily. He grabbed Rachel and me by the elbow and guided us in the direction of a neon sign that said "Submarine Sandwiches." My first instinct was to punch him and run, but I knew that if I stormed off now, Rachel would be mad at me. Her hat was on crooked, and there was this look of glazed wonder on her face.

"Oh, okay," I said with bad grace.

"I didn't even know you knew Hedrick, Andie," said P.J. "He's so stuffy he makes my dad look cool. I am not kidding you."

"Did you see the way he was drooling over her?" Chris asked.

"Disgusting," agreed P.J. "He ought to stick with girls who are as stuffy as he is."

"I *am* as stuffy as he is," I said firmly. "I also want to run my life totally without interference, if you don't mind. That's why I got Rachel to give me a ride to the mall tonight instead of you guys. I never expected you three to show up and ruin everything for me."

"Who? Us? Did we interfere?" asked P.J.

"She seems to think so," said Chris.

"We're truly sorry. Aren't we sorry, Chris?"

"Deeply. Profoundly."

"I told you she was gonna be mad," said Dooley. "I thought we were supposed to be out here celebrating, not scaring off stupid Hedrick."

"Hey-hey!" said Chris. "Get this, Andie. Our Dooley is now a licensed driver."

Embarrassed, Dooley laid his shiny laminated card out on the table for me to admire. The small I.D. photo in the left corner looked like that of a poisoner caught in the act, but if I had one of those licenses, I wouldn't care *how* awful my picture was.

"Congratulations, Dooley." I gulped. I was realizing that if I had a driver's license, I wouldn't have had to go after Hedrick, who come to think of it did look somewhat stuffy. I was really annoyed at the way he had disappeared without so much as a goodbye. Where did a girl have to go to find a guy who wouldn't be scared off by Chris and P.J.?

"Did you have any trouble with the driving test?" Rachel asked.

Dooley snapped his fingers. "Easy as pie."

"The only thing I had trouble with was the parallel parking," said Rachel.

"Practice, you gotta practice. That's the secret," Dooley said modestly. "Of course, I've been driving since I was ten, unofficially."

"Anybody want to split a sub with me?" asked Chris. "What about you, Rache?"

Rachel looked down so that her face was completely hidden by her hat. She had evidently lost all power of speech.

"We just had ice cream," I explained. "We aren't hungry."

"Hey, you aren't still mad at us, are you, Andie?" Chris leaned his chin on his fist and tried to look sincere. It was a pathetic attempt. "Look, if it bothers you, we won't do it again, will we, P.J.?"

"Andie knows we're only trying to help her out," said P.J.

"Wait a minute," I protested.

"But all you have to do is say the word, and we'll let you be," P.J. said.

"Yeah, consider it done." Chris and P.J. exchanged smiles.

I knew an empty promise when I heard one. I stared at the neon outline of a sub. Life was black.

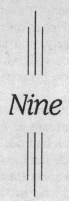

Nine

When we got back to Rachel's house, she was in a daze. "He touched me," she kept saying. "Chris touched me. I may never wash this arm. Did you hear him? He asked if I wanted to split a sub with him!"

"Rachel, I don't understand why you've got this thing about Chris. He's just a guy. What does he have that lots of other guys don't have?"

She looked at me in amazement. "Where do you want me to begin?"

"I can't believe," I said, "that you are so shallow that all you care about is looks. What happened to character, sensitivity, intelligence? What about those things?"

"Time enough for all that stuff when I get old." Rachel pulled off her shoes and tossed her hat on the bed. "Besides, it's not just his looks, Andie."

97

She lay down on some crumpled clothes and stared dreamily off into space. "It's something about him. He looks like he's having so much fun. It's like I just want to join the party, you know?" She got up suddenly. "Could you wait while I wash my hair? You do remember you promised to braid it, don't you?"

I remembered. Unfortunately. And to think I hadn't exchanged so many as fifty words with Jim Hedrick. Talk about a bad deal.

There wasn't much for me to do while Rachel washed her hair. If I spent the time trying to clean her room, she would have had a fit. She continued to insist that if everything was just left where it was, she could find it.

I noticed she had added another name to her wall chart. "Elise Simmons." Who the heck was Elise Simmons? And who even cared? I saw the futility of human endeavor so clearly just at that moment— girls chasing boys, boys chasing girls, yet nobody ever catching anybody they wanted.

At last I heard the shower stop. Rachel kicked open the door to her bathroom with a bare foot. Her hair was wrapped in a white towel.

"You want me to braid it wet?" I asked.

"Absolutely. That way I'll get two looks for one. First I'll have the cornrows, and when I unbraid them it'll be crimped."

I found Rachel's comb and started to work. Rachel's black hair came below her shoulderblades, and cornrows, needless to say, were not the work of a moment.

"Stand still," I said. "This is very tricky work."

"My neck is stiff."

"Be quiet. You're throwing me all off. An artist must have quiet in order to concentrate." I prided myself on my cornrows.

"Now my neck is really stiff," Rachel said a little while later. "I know I said it was stiff before, but that was just a preview to the incredible stiffness I'm getting now. Has anybody ever been left with a permanent disability from having her hair put in cornrows?"

"Not as far as I know," I said shortly. "Now be still."

"You're just mad because that thing with Jim Hedrick didn't come off, aren't you?"

"Mad? Of course I'm mad. What do you think? How would you like to be treated like P.J.'s chattel or something?"

"P.J.'s chattel, no." She tilted her head reflectively. "But Chris's chattel, yummy."

"You are sick. Straighten your head."

I looped the braids around in loose coils all over her head and secured them. If I said so myself, that hair was a work of art. Even more important, it was finished.

"Let me see." Rachel jumped up and pulled off the sweatshirt that was hanging over her mirror so she could see herself. She preened, pouted her lips, raised her eyebrows, and puffed out her chest. "I like it," she concluded. "It's exotic, wild, and dangerous. It's definitely me."

I had doubts about it being definitely her, but it did seem likely it would help Chris notice her, which was what she wanted.

"The only thing is," she said thoughtfully, "I'm not sure my hat will go over it."

"Rachel! You don't wear a painter's hat with cornrows! It would ruin the whole effect!"

"Just let me try it and see how it looks."

"It's an insult to my art," I muttered.

But she kept pawing through the clothes piled on her bed. "I thought I left it right here."

"Have you ever thought of giving this place a cleaning once a decade or so?"

"No," she said shortly. "I told you I like it just the way it is. I know where everything is."

Sure. She knew where everything was and she and Chris were perfectly matched and I was Daffy Duck.

Then I spotted something in the guinea pig cage. It looked sort of like Rachel's hat. I watched it uneasily out of the corner of my eye, not wanting to be the one to break the news to her.

She saw it finally. "My hat!" she screeched. She tenderly scooped it up with both hands. The guinea pig skittered over to a corner and chattered his teeth threateningly. "My hat!" Rachel stared at it with bleary-eyed disbelief.

A web of white the shape of a bowl and a ruffled-looking bill was all that remained of the hat. It was almost lacy. The bill of the hat, which was thicker and harder to chew than the rest of the hat, had apparently baffled the guinea pig, and he had nibbled only the edges of it. Most of the rest of it was gone. The guinea pig had had plenty of time to work on it while Rachel was shampooing and while I was doing the cornrows.

Rachel slid to the floor and sat there, her face streaked with tears. I watched her unhappily.

"You could get another one?" I suggested.

"That hat belonged to my grandfather!" she sobbed.

"I guess it was very special."

"Special! It was my trademark. It was a part of me." She glanced at it again and burst into fresh tears.

"Don't look at it, Rachel." I laid the towel over it. "It's better that way."

"Maybe it could be fixed," she said with a sudden tremor of hopefulness. "It could be rewoven. You know, like they do with coats that have a moth hole? They reweave them."

The trouble was there was more hole than hat at this point. Anyway, I had never heard of reweaving a painter's hat.

"I can't stand it." She buried her face in her hands. "I can't go on. How can I live without my hat? This is the most awful thing that has ever happened to me. My poor h-h-hat—"

"I'm awfully sorry," I said uncomfortably. "Well, I guess I'd better be going, now." I edged toward the door.

"Don't leave me!" she cried.

"Rachel, it's just a hat!"

She snuffled loudly. "I know that. Of course I know that. You know, tomorrow I'm going to call this guy Mom knows who does restorations for museums. Maybe he can fix it."

"Maybe you could just get a hat that's exactly like it."

"There isn't any hat that's exactly like it. You don't understand. This was *my* hat. It has a history. It's part of my life. My own special hat." She got too choked up to speak.

"Look, Rachel, I'm awfully, awfully sorry, but it's ten o'clock and I've got to get home. Maybe you ought to take two aspirin and try to get some sleep, huh?"

"I may never sleep again," she said tragically.

If it were even a stuffed animal, I could almost understand it. I was quite attached to Finnegan. But a hat? I had seen people on the news who had their houses swept away by a hurricane, and they held themselves together better than Rachel was doing. Of course, it was sad. I knew she loved that stupid hat. I hated to go and leave her by herself, but there really wasn't anything I could do.

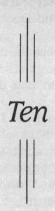

Ten

Tuesday, at school, Rachel seemed to be a different person, not just because she was hatless, but because she was so subdued. And of course her hair was spectacular with these shining black loops framing her large violet eyes.

I happened to be sitting with the guys when she came into the cafeteria at lunch.

"My God, who's that?" said Chris.

The note of interest in his voice alarmed me. Suddenly I realized I didn't want anything to change. My intuition screeched "Stop!" "I believe she's an Israeli exchange student," I said quickly. "She's going back to her own country at the end of the week, and I understand her English isn't that great."

"That can't be right. There's something awfully

103

familiar about her," Chris said, puzzled. "I can't put my finger on it. Maybe it's the way she walks."

"That's Rachel," said Dooley's froggy voice. "I recognize her shoes."

"Nah, Rachel? Rachel, the next-door neighbor?" P.J. looked incredulous.

"What happened to that dumb hat of hers?" asked Chris.

"Don't ask her about it," I warned him. Chris was already speaking in the soft, reverent voice that I recognized as indicating that another of his three-day crushes was beginning. The problem was that having been around to witness Rachel's reaction to the loss of her hat, I wasn't at all sure I wanted to be around when she first won and then lost Chris.

"Rachel!" Chris yelled.

I had a funny cold feeling in the bottom of my stomach when Rachel came over to our table. This was it. She was going to get her wish. I felt like a helpless bystander about to witness a car crash.

"Hi," Rachel said shyly. Her eyes were shadowed, probably because she was thinking about her hat. But nobody else seemed to notice. Chris leaned back and pulled out a chair for her. "Where have you been all my life?" he said.

"What did you say?" She looked confused. No wonder.

P.J. had just picked up his sloppy joe. "Hey, Rache, what happened to your—"

I kicked him so hard he choked.

"You shouldn't talk with your mouth open," I observed sweetly.

He looked at me in amazement.

"On't-day alk-tay bout-ay at-hay!" I warned him in a hoarse pig Latin.

"Whah?" P.J. looked bewildered.

It was probably silly of me to worry about P.J.'s mentioning the hat. Quite possibly Rachel wouldn't have noticed anything more subtle than a major earthquake. She was practically nose to nose with Chris, and he was talking fast and soft. She looked dazed. I only hoped she wasn't agreeing to anything illegal, immoral, or fattening. The girl was not in a normal state of mind and could not be held responsible.

A boy came up to our table waving a handful of cardboard squares. "Tickets to the dance, anybody? It's for a good cause. Come on, come on, let's support Beta Club's Falling Leaves Dance. What do you say?"

"I'll take two," said Chris. While reaching in his wallet, he never once took his eyes off Rachel. I noticed that her violet eyes were moist and her lips were slightly parted. In my opinion she looked as if she weren't quite bright, which, as far as Chris was concerned, was true enough. I could just imagine the state of her respiration because I had gotten a few of those looks from Chris myself.

"You can give me a couple of those tickets, too," P.J. said casually.

Chris was so busy hitting on Rachel that he didn't even notice P.J. buying the tickets, but I grasped the full significance of it at once. Almost every weekend, P.J. went to one of the big outdoor bashes he was so fond of, the ones with hundreds of people, midnight swims, illegal kegs. That was his idea of "going out and having a good time." Was he now actually paying good money for the privilege of getting dressed up to go somewhere and *behave?* Dooley and I exchanged a glance. This could be serious.

As soon as lunch was over, I rushed to my next class, but Rachel caught up with me and grabbed my sleeve. "Wait a minute, Andie."

"I can't afford to be late again," I said. "It causes too much wear and tear on my nervous system."

"Don't you even want to know what Chris said to me?"

"Sure," I said politely. "Of course I do. Naturally."

"He asked me to the Falling Leaves Dance!"

"Gee, that's great, Rache. I'm really happy for you." Actually, my heart bled for her, but it would hardly have been tactful to say so. Poor misguided soul. As if there was any "right way" to be Chris's girlfriend except to resign yourself to a reign of three days or so. Rachel just couldn't seem to grasp that.

She plucked at my sleeve. "Andie, you've got to go to the dance, too."

I detached her fingers. "Calm down, Rache."

"You can't leave me all alone! What am I going to do? I'm so nervous. I've never even been out with a boy, not a real boy, that is, unless you count Michael Hargrave asking me to the ninth-grade picnic, and that doesn't really count. I'm just so nervous!" She bit her lip. "I mean, to start out with

Chris! It's like skipping the bunny slopes and going straight to the Olympics."

"You'll be fine. What are you worried about? This is the answer to your dreams, right?"

"What do you *mean,* what am I worried about? I don't want to do anything *wrong.*" Her eyes pleaded with me. "You know that. I've got to think about this. I've got to plan it down to the last detail. I'd better practice what I'm going to say." She stiffened suddenly. "Yes, that's it. Planning is the key. I need a script."

"It might be better to be spontaneous."

"You see?" she implored me. "That's the kind of input I need. Just having you around will make me feel more secure. You do understand that, don't you? I mean, now that my hat is gone," she swallowed, "my confidence isn't what it was. I need your help!"

"Rachel, I'd do anything for you. Anything within reason, but I will not go alone to a major formal dance. I just won't."

"Can't you get somebody to ask you?"

I looked at her pityingly. Hadn't she noticed that I had been trying to get something going with a boy for weeks and with absolutely no results, thanks to P.J. and his friends? "I don't see how. I've got to go now, Rache. Really."

As I dashed off to class, I found myself worrying about Rachel. I couldn't pretend she was the sort who rolled with the punches, not after that business with the hat. She was right—a little support the night of the dance might make all the difference. If

Chris ricocheted to the side of some blonde before the evening was over, I would need to be at hand to apply cold compresses to her brow. What kind of friend was I? Of course, the fact is it wasn't that I wasn't willing to help out. I just couldn't figure out how.

That afternoon as I was trekking to the west parking lot, I noticed that P.J. had already gotten to the car and was leaning his rear against the grill. In front of him stood a short girl with a cloud of curly blond hair. Judging from the sappy smile on P.J.'s face, I figured the girl had to be Susie.

"That's Susie," croaked Dooley, confirming my suspicions. He had fallen into step beside me. Dooley never had much to say, but right at the moment he seemed even more silent and morose than usual.

Suddenly I stopped dead in my tracks and stared at him. I had a wonderful idea. Dooley had a car and a driver's license. Furthermore, Dooley was a guy that Chris and P.J. could not scare away. *He* could take me to the dance. The beauty and simplicity of it all took my breath away. "Dooley," I said, "how would you like to go to the Falling Leaves Dance?"

"Huh?"

"I'll buy the tickets," I said. "My treat. Wouldn't it be fun?"

"Nope."

"Oh, come on, Dooley! Help me out! Rachel's supposed to go with Chris, and she's scared out of her mind. She wants me to be there to hold her hand."

"Let Chris hold her hand," he said sourly.

"I need to be there to offer her moral support. Just do me this favor."

He hunched his shoulders up and scowled. "Okay."

I was a little thrown by his giving in so suddenly. It was like picking up a can expecting it to be heavy and finding out it's empty. I hadn't expected him to give in so easily, and it worried me. I wondered what it meant, but his face was unreadable. Those shoe-button black eyes stared straight ahead.

"It's just because I need to do this favor for Rachel, you see," I explained carefully. I certainly didn't want Dooley to think I was getting romantic about him.

"I get it, I get it."

"Then it's all set?" I asked. "We're going to go to the Falling Leaves Dance?"

"Okay, but I'm not going to dress up," he said. "Forget that."

I decided to quit looking a gift horse in the mouth. If Dooley had agreed to go with me without any fuss, that was all to the good. What was I worrying about? My problem was solved. I couldn't wait to tell Rachel it was all set.

The next day at school P.J. saw me buying the tickets to the dance. "I hope whoever you're going with has a car," he said, "because Susie and I want to be alone. And I mean *alone.*"

"Don't worry," I said. "It's Dooley I'm going with. We'll take his Jeep." I stuffed the tickets in my billfold.

"Dooley? You're going with Dooley?"

"I don't suppose you have any objection to that, do you? I mean he's not a dork, he doesn't belong to the Young Republicans Club. In fact, he is one of the gang," I finished triumphantly.

"Yeah, but I didn't know that you and Dooley—"

"It's just a dance, P.J. I'm not marrying him or anything. Take a chill pill."

I strode off, satisfied that I had, for once, left him at a loss for words.

When I went over to Rachel's house Saturday night, she was working on the script for her date with Chris.

"My feeling is that the less I say, the better," she said. "That way there's less opportunity for me to mess up."

"Whatever you say."

"Look, Andie, I value your suggestions. Don't just humor me, okay? You know Chris. You can give me a lot of good pointers."

She spread a newspaper out on the bed. "I've been reading up on football. I checked out a book from the library. As far as I can tell, football is sort of a cross between chess and war, but it's extremely complicated, and I don't think I can learn enough about it to say anything intelligent by next weekend."

I thought she was probably right. Not that I had

ever noticed the guys themselves saying anything intelligent about football. It was mostly, "How about those Tarheels, hey? Way to go!"

"Aren't you and Chris going out tonight?" I asked.

"No, he's at his grandparents' fiftieth anniversary celebration, thank goodness. Because now that this has happened, Andie, now that he's actually noticed me, I can see that I'm not at all ready." She clasped her hands and held them over her heart. "I mean, after all the times I had dreamed of this, yesterday at lunch when he talked to me, everything just went out of my mind—*whoosh*. I sat there like I was in a trance or something."

"That's okay. Chris is the shallow type that just goes for looks anyway."

"Do you have to keep putting Chris down?" she snapped.

"Sorry."

"You're always trying to discourage me. This is tricky enough without somebody filling me with negative thoughts. Now, I'm going to skip lunch next week so I don't have to risk running into him. I'll just take an apple and a sandwich to school and eat it under the stairs on A wing. I don't want to say *anything* that's going to ruin this. I need to *think*. I need to plan."

"Do you really think that you can plan these things?"

"Maybe not." She looked at me thoughtfully. "Do you think Zen meditation would help?"

I shrugged.

"Well, what about a lucky rabbit's foot? I saw one

111

advertised in a magazine, but I'm not sure it would get here in time."

"On second thought," I said, "I'd go with the script."

That night, close to one in the morning, I was in the kitchen warming a cup of milk in the microwave in the hope of curing my insomnia. I've always had a problem with waking up in the middle of the night and thinking and then not being able to go back to sleep. Right at that moment I was thinking about what Rachel had said. Maybe she was right and I was wrong. Maybe this would be the all-time great romance. My mother had always told me that hard work and perseverance would pay off, and Rachel had certainly worked and persevered. She had practically turned her yearning for Chris into a profession.

The only sound in the kitchen just then was the hum of the refrigerator and the faint whirl of the kitchen clock. Then the kitchen door opened stealthily.

My heart jumped up in my throat and stayed there, pounding. I grabbed at the butcher knife, but a half second later P.J. stepped into the kitchen. Every bit of his hair had turned to cowlicks, as if he had been frantically scrambling it with his fingers. I felt pretty silly when I recognized him. Relieved, but silly.

"Do you have to sneak in like that?" I said sharply. I put the knife back in the rack. "I didn't even hear you coming up the steps." I frowned. "In fact, I didn't hear your car, either." I went over to the door, opened it again, and looked downstairs. P.J.'s car wasn't in the garage.

I stared at him. "What happened? Did you wreck the Camaro?"

P.J. was leaning against the counter, breathing deeply. At first he didn't speak, and I was getting pretty alarmed. He slid down into a kitchen chair as if he no longer trusted his knees to hold him. "Dooley and Chris gave me a ride."

"But where's your car?" I corrected myself. "I mean, *our* car."

"I had to leave it at Shaun's house. Where are Dad and Ellen?" He looked jumpy, as if he expected them to pop out from behind a curtain any second.

"They're in bed, naturally. It's after one. Why did you leave the car at Shaun's? What's wrong? Why are you skulking around like this? What happened, P.J.?"

"Well, you remember how Dad was telling us about the police telling people to leave that party at Mike's and then just picking them up for DUI? It almost happened to me."

"Have you been drinking?"

"I'd nursed one beer all night. Do you know whether one beer would show up on a breathalyzer test?"

I shrugged. Happily, this was not the kind of information I had ever needed.

"Well, you see the way it was with me. I couldn't risk getting into that car. When that cop stood up in the middle of the party and yelled that we had to clear out in ten minutes, I thought about the way they raked in the kids at that last party, and I knew I'd better not try to drive. You heard what Dad said about 'no car—ever' if the cops raked me in." He shuddered. "So I walked to a convenience store about a mile or so away and called Dooley, but his line was busy. I guess he had knocked the phone off the hook. So then I had to call Chris. He sneaked out and went over to Dooley's house to get him and then they both came and got me. I'm going to have to go back tomorrow and get the Camaro. Dooley's going to come get me at dawn and take me back to Shaun's house. I just want to get it back in the garage before Dad wakes up. What if he catches me driving in at six A.M., Andie? Give me some perfectly logical reason why I would be driving in at six A.M."

"There isn't any logical reason. You'd just better not get caught."

"That's kinda what I thought." P.J. got up. "I'm going to set my alarm and put it under my pillow so when it goes off I can shut it off right away and Dad and Ellen won't hear it."

"But what if Dooley forgets to set his alarm?"

"Then I'll just walk down to his house and get him. Well, good night." He tried a smile, but it didn't quite come off. He seemed as close to unglued as I had ever seen him.

After he left, I sat there in my bathrobe finishing my hot milk in peace, glad that escaping from the police did not figure into my idea of Saturday-night fun.

Eleven

"Chris and Rachel are going to double with us," Dooley told me the following Thursday.

This is good, I thought. I'll be able to offer moral support to Rachel right from the beginning.

The previous afternoon, when I was over at her house, I had noticed that her famous wall chart had been taken down. Now what was taped up over the bed were several rows of flimsy computer paper.

"I decided having the chart up was bad luck," Rachel explained. "I don't want to act as if I'm expecting to put up a card with my own name on it and a note showing how I messed up." She licked her lips nervously.

"I didn't know you were superstitious."

"I didn't know it myself, but all of a sudden I'm knocking on wood and running from black cats."

She looked anxious. "Do you think that indicates a fatal lack of confidence?"

"Oh, I don't know." The answer was self-evident —poor Rachel was a nervous wreck. But why make her feel worse? I needed to build her up, not tear her down. I began to feel like a trainer sending a particularly inexperienced fighter into the ring. "You'll be fine," I said in soothing tones. "Just fine."

"I don't want to be fine, I want to be perfect. I want Chris to be swept away by the transports of everlasting love. I want him to crave my bod."

I glanced at her quickly, but she was showing no other obvious signs of delirium. "Sure," I said. "Sure you do."

She pointed at the computer paper. "My scripts!"

I stood up on the bed to read them. I wouldn't have stood up on just anybody's bed, but the way Rachel kept her room, respect for her possessions seemed ridiculous. Skimming the scripts, I saw she had provided alternative versions for the evening's conversation. For example, on one she had Chris beginning the conversation by saying, "Nice weather we're having." On another she had him say, "You look ravishing, Rachel." Neither of these lines seemed like anything Chris would say, but at least she was trying to build a little flexibility into her system and that was good.

"If you have any suggestions," she said, "don't hesitate."

"Well, I don't think Chris would actually say 'Nice weather we're having.' And are you really going to just talk about the refreshments and the decorations? I mean, I just can't picture it somehow, Rachel. You always have such interesting things to say."

"You don't think it's okay?" she asked, downcast. "I asked my mother to help me with it."

"You mean your mother knows all about these scripts? You're kidding me!"

Rachel cast a glance at the door. "No, of course not. I just asked her what to talk about at the dance, and she said that when in doubt you can always talk about the decorations and the refreshments."

"Sounds awfully boring."

"I know. I never thought I'd be taking my mother's advice. That just shows you how desperate I am."

"You ought to try to relax."

"Easy to say. This is the moment I've waited for, planned for, hoped for— By the way, can you put my hair in cornrows for the dance?"

The phone rang and Rachel groped for it under some trash. At last she found the receiver. "Hello? This is Rachel. Wait a minute. She's right here."

She handed me the phone.

"Andie?" said a deep voice.

I had a sudden sinking feeling. It was Thursday afternoon and I was supposed to be at Pete Joyner's to work on the history project. How could I have forgotten again? "I'm sorry, Pete. I'm on my way. Honestly." I slammed the receiver down. "Rachel, I need a ride over to Pete Joyner's. I was supposed to be there ages ago."

She stood up and slipped on her shoes. "Isn't this the second time you've stood the poor sucker up?"

"I haven't stood him up. I'm just running a little bit late, that's all."

"What about the cornrows? Do I have your promise on that?"

I could see that if I was going to be dependent on Rachel for transportation I would be spending a lot of time braiding her hair. "Yes, yes, I'll do it," I said. "Let's go."

This was so embarrassing! How could I forget to meet Pete two times? Perhaps there was some deep subconscious instinct warning me to stay away from guys who could pick me up with one arm.

It turned out that Pete Joyner lived in a colonial house only a mile or so from my house. As soon as he came to the door, Rachel drove off and left me alone with him. Well, what did I expect anyway? For her to stay and be my bodyguard?

"Hi," I said. Suddenly self-conscious, I scuffed the toe of my shoe against the porch. "I'm awfully sorry I'm late."

"Hey, come on in. I've got something for you," he said. When I followed him inside, he loomed over me, but I could hear clinking dishes in the kitchen. That was reassuring. Pete might be pretty annoyed at me for being an hour late, but I figured he wasn't likely to actually hit me as long as his mother was in the next room.

I sank down into a chair and practically disappeared into it. It was oversize. Everything in the room was oversize—the couch, the chairs. Something told me this family did not own a compact car.

Pete got a small package off the couch and handed it to me.

"For me?" I asked weakly. I pulled off the flimsy pink wrapping paper. "An appointment book." I looked at him uneasily. "How did you know I didn't have one?"

"Lucky guess." He smiled at me.

When he smiled I could see there was a slight space between his two front teeth and that surprised me. Perhaps I had expected fangs. Also I kept expecting him to say things like "Me hungry. Want blood." Instead I got this stuff about appointment calendars.

This was a guy who was well-organized to the core. Not only was he starting on his history project weeks ahead of time, he already had some of his work spread out on the dining room table. I followed him over to the table.

"This is what I've got so far," he said.

I blushed. I was aware that the history project had not been high on my list of priorities. In fact, most of the time I forgot all about it. Lately I seemed to spend all my time thinking about the upcoming Falling Leaves Dance and Rachel's date with Chris. Would she survive? Would I? Probably Pete was cursing the day Miss Wrigley had paired us off, and I couldn't exactly blame him.

"I mean, I hope you don't mind," he went on pointedly. "I just wanted to start."

"I'm sorry I haven't helped yet. But I'm here now

and extremely eager to get to work. Honestly I am."
I did my best to look eager.

When I leafed through the notes on the table, I saw that what he had so far wasn't exactly earth-shaking. The most exciting events from the early town history were "Founding of the First Method-ist Church," and "Railroad Comes to Town."

"Somebody's already doing the railroad," I pointed out.

Pete shook his head. "We don't have a lot of possibilities."

"It's just too bad George Washington never slept here," I said. "Or if even Lafayette had stopped over to feed his horses or something, we would at least have something. As far as I can tell, nothing has ever happened here. I think maybe we're going to have to go to the library and do a lot more digging."

"I guess you're right." Pete went to the dining room door and called, "Mom, we're going to the library." He pulled his keys out of his pocket as we walked toward the door. "Have you heard about the Falling Leaves Dance on Saturday?" he asked.

"Yes, and I'm even going to it. But I don't think there's a historical angle to it. The signs said Third Annual Dance. I don't think Miss Wrigley would call three years history."

He looked taken aback. "No, I guess not," he said.

"Not that I want to slap down your ideas," I added. "We've got to turn over every stone if we're going to come up with something new. The founding of the First Methodist Church is just not something we can get a class presentation out of. At least, I don't think we can."

Pete's car was one of Detroit's more massive products. It had so much leg room you could have played soccer under the dashboard.

"Didn't I hear somebody say that you're P.J.'s stepsister?" asked Pete after we got in.

"Yes, P.J. and I are related, strange as it may seem."

He laughed. "I know what you're saying. You two aren't much alike." He put the car in reverse and backed out of the driveway. "P.J.'s sort of a party guy. Kind of wild, isn't he?"

"Well, I have my own quiet thrills, you know. Letting my library books get overdue—"

"And missing study dates," he finished. I was relieved to see that he was still smiling.

When we got to the library, we spent an hour going through the most boring trivia, but finally I had a blinding inspiration. I slapped *The History of Westmarket* closed, causing everybody in the room to jump. "I've got it!" I whispered jubilantly. "We can do a history of Grouman's Department Stores! Forget all this library stuff. We can interview Richard, my stepfather. It will be primary research. Miss Wrigley will love it."

"That's a really good idea." Pete looked at me in admiration.

Well, it *was* a good idea. I felt proud.

"That's settled then," I said. It was just as well I finally came up with an idea because it was supper-time and I was getting hungry. Also I needed more time to think about how I could build Rachel's self-confidence.

"Maybe we ought to meet next week to plan our strategy," he suggested.

"Oh, I don't think so. Now that we've got our idea, it's just a matter of wrapping it up. I'll talk to Richard and let you know if I run into any snag."

He looked disappointed. Some people are gluttons for work, and obviously Pete was one of them. He drove me back to Rocky Knoll and dropped me off at my house. The garage door was open. When I went in, I saw that Dooley was working out on the NordicTrack. "Yo, Dooley," I said perfunctorily. I mounted the stairs to the kitchen.

"Hey, hold up, Andie. I want to talk."

I stared at Dooley in alarm. I was beginning to wonder if I'd made a mistake asking him to take me to the dance. I felt I had been crystal clear about my going only as a favor to Rachel, but very possibly we had a slight communication problem. It was going to be extremely awkward if he got a crush on me. I might have to get P.J. to reiterate that stuff about my being a civilian. "You, ah, want to talk?" I inquired cautiously.

Dooley got off the track, came over, and sat down on the steps beneath me. A terry-cloth band wrapped around his forehead kept his hair out of his eyes. "Yeah, you know like I want to get the female point of view, you know?"

"I'm female, all right," I admitted grudgingly. "But exactly what do you have in mind?"

"Like, what if a person likes a girl, like, and she

doesn't know it?" He seemed to be embarrassed. "What do you think, like, a person ought to do?"

I swallowed. Could he possibly be talking about me? The things I got into to help my friends!

"Maybe you ought to watch for signs that she might be interested in you." I coughed uncomfortably. *"Very* clear signs."

He frowned. "That doesn't make any sense. Somebody's got to make the first move, right?"

Yes, I thought, suddenly frozen with fear. And I have. I asked you to take me to the dance! I must have been out of my mind. The problem was that though I *liked* Dooley, I just couldn't envision him as the love interest in my life. It was a delicate situation. I couldn't think of what to do about it except get out of there really fast before he said something embarrassing. "I don't have time to talk right now, Dooley," I said. "I've got to work on my history project."

His melancholy black eyes followed me reproachfully as I went on inside.

Twelve

My mother was very excited about the Falling Leaves Dance. She loved dances, maybe because they were a staple of her fiction. She pictured dances complete with princes in disguise and men with black patches over one eye. At the sort of dance Mom had in mind, a beautiful woman with an empty life went out on the balcony one night and thought of ending it all by diving off a cliff into the foaming waves, but then a dark stranger appeared and swept her into a fascinating and dangerous adventure that gave her a reason to live. Mom didn't actually say these were her expectations for me for the Falling Leaves Dance, but I hadn't been her daughter for almost sixteen years for nothing. I could read between the lines.

"We're going to have to get you a marvelous new dress!" she said, her eyes beginning to shine.

I felt I should inject a note of reality. "It's Dooley I'm going with, Mom. Remember Dooley? And I'm only going to help Rachel out. She said she'd feel better if I was there."

"But that's the thing about dances, Andie. Anything can happen. With all the lights and the decorations, the atmosphere is charged with magic. Cinderella's pumpkin becomes a golden carriage. Ordinary boys start to look dashing and glamorous." Mom lifted herself lightly on her toes. "You'll see. Amazing things can happen."

What could I say? On some level my mom actually believes in the stuff she writes.

Later on she came into my room and offered me a compact full of glitter that she called "body diamonds." "Just a touch," she sang. "Something special for a special evening."

"I don't think so," I said.

She looked a little hurt. "I just want you to enjoy your youth, darling. Sometimes I think you've had to grow up too fast, with losing your father and all. This should be a time for you to have fun!"

I've noticed that whatever a kid does, his parents never like it. Look at P.J. He was out having fun all the time exactly the way Mom thought I should, but Richard wasn't happy about it. Nothing seems to satisfy parents.

I had intended to braid Rachel's hair during the afternoon on Saturday so as to avoid any last-minute rush, but she wasn't home once the whole day. Every time I called her, Mrs. Green told me she was still out shopping.

I got a bulletin on Rachel's state of mind at four that afternoon when she called from a pay phone to tell me she was undecided about whether the red strapless looked better than the emerald satin. "I thought you already had your dress," I said, "and I thought it was pink."

"I did have one, but I took it back this morning. I had serious second thoughts. It looked sweet, and I realized I want to look exotic, exciting, and dangerous."

"Try black leather and whips."

"That isn't funny, Andie. I'm really in the throes of indecision here. It's funny because I don't normally have trouble making up my mind. It's like my will is paralyzed. Come to the mall and help me decide."

"I can't drive, remember? Do you want me to find P.J.? I could explain the situation to him and ask him to give me a ride."

"Golly, no!" she shrieked. "He might say something to Chris. What an awful thought! Just forget it." She hung up abruptly.

I saw Rachel going in her front door later that afternoon. She was carrying a large dress box, so she had obviously finally decided on a dress. The whole thing was ridiculous. I expect there are nuclear nonproliferation treaties that get signed with a lot less deliberation than Rachel was spending on a single date with Chris.

As soon as we finished supper at our house, I went over to the Greens'. Mrs. Green let me in, and I went right up to Rachel's room. I found her sitting in her underwear at her dressing table. She was carefully applying mascara to her jet-black lashes. "Do you know how to bead eyelashes?" she asked.

"Honestly, Rache, don't you want Chris to be able to see the real you?"

"No, I want him to fall wildly and passionately in love with me."

Silly question.

I got the comb and set to work. "Something smells funny in here." I sniffed suspiciously. I had always suspected that someday something would get lost under the mess in Rachel's room and start to decay. It was the sort of room where I wouldn't have been a bit surprised to see a toadstool growing out of a light socket. There were parts of it that were more untouched than wilderness areas in major national forests. But somehow what I smelled was not the smell of decay. It was more medicinal than that. "Did you spill spot remover maybe?"

"Nope," said Rachel. "Never touch the stuff." She lifted the tumbler on her dressing table and took a long swig. The smell grew stronger.

I stared. "Rachel, you're drinking!"

"I'm just trying to calm myself down some. I got a bottle out of my dad's liquor cabinet. He has every kind of thing." She pulled a sapphire-blue bottle from under the skirt of the dressing table and squinted at it. "It's gin," she said, "I had to hold my nose at first, but now I guess my tongue is sort of numb. It tastes terrible, but I'm a lot more relaxed already."

I took the bottle from her hands. She was so

relaxed she didn't even seem to notice. "This is a bad idea, Rachel. Trust me," I said. "You should relax by thinking beautiful thoughts or by taking long walks."

She rested her chin on her hand. "The only beautiful thought I can think of is Chris falling wildly, passionately in love with me."

"You do understand what I'm saying, don't you, Rache?" I spoke slowly and kindly, as if to a small child. "It's a bad idea."

She waved her hand. "Sure. I'm plenty relaxed enough now anyway. Now that I think of it, my head feels sort of funny. Like it's floating, you know?"

I went into the bathroom and poured the whole bottle down the sink.

"I've never actually had anything to drink before," Rachel said when I began braiding again. "It's very strange. It's hard to believe people do it for fun. It tastes so awful and it feels so funny. On the other hand, undoubt"—she hesitated then continued with more confidence—"indubitably, it is relaxing." She laid her head down on her arm.

"You have to hold your head up," I said, "if I'm going to braid your hair."

"Oh, phooey." She smiled a dippy little smile into the mirror but managed to hold her head up.

She was very quiet while I worked on her hair. Every now and then she smiled.

"I think you'd better eat some crackers or something," I said uneasily. "They might sort of soak it up, you know."

"Sure," she said.

The guinea pig cowered in a corner of his cage and chattered his teeth.

Finally I finished the braiding and began looping the braids up and securing them. "Don't forget to eat those crackers," I reminded her.

"Sure," she said.

It was pretty obvious she was not herself, but I figured the liquor was bound to wear off. By the time we were all dressed and ready to go, I hoped Rachel would be normal again.

I went home and put on my marvelous new dress, a sleek jade satin. For a second after I put it on, I was seized with the insane impulse to waltz around the room singing "Some Day My Prince Will Come." I would be getting as romantic as my mother if I wasn't careful.

Dooley called at seven-thirty. His froggy voice floated over the wire like bad static. "The Jeep's got a flat," he said. "And we can't use my dad's car because he's off visiting one of his girlfriends. And I can't use the spare because the spare is already on it."

"Oh, dear. Is it all off then?" Suddenly my heart felt light. I smiled broadly into the phone. I was saved. I wouldn't have to worry about Dooley getting a crush on me. I wouldn't have to worry about Rachel being too relaxed. There are times when an evening with a library book sounds like heaven and as far as I was concerned this was one of them.

"Not to worry," said Dooley. "Let me talk to P.J."

"It's no good, Dooley. He won't give us a ride. He wants to be alone with Susie."

"Look, I got up in the middle of the night to save P.J.'s neck last weekend. Now it's his turn. So don't give me that."

I covered the receiver with my hand and yelled for P.J. He came thundering down the stairs. "What is it, Andie? Can't you see I'm getting dressed?"

He was wearing red suspenders and his hair was slicked down as if it had been shellacked. I stared at him in amazement. This must have been what my mom meant when she talked about the amazing transformation brought about by dances. P.J. looked like the toy groom on a wedding cake.

"What are you staring at?" P.J. snarled.

"Nothing," I said. "Nothing at all. Dooley wants to talk to you." I handed him the phone and fled.

My mom heard me coming upstairs and stuck her head out of her bedroom. "Need any help getting ready, darling? Oh, don't you look lovely! Like a princess. Hang on, I want to get a picture."

The next thing I knew I was seeing blue dots. I steadied myself against the nearest wall. P.J. passed me, snarling and talking to himself. "Sure, I can give everybody and his brother a ride. What am I, a taxi service? You get a chance to be alone, and this is what happens."

Richard appeared at the head of the stairs. "Anything the matter, son?"

P.J. stiffened. "No, sir!"

Richard beamed at me. "Don't you look nice,

Andie! You take after your mother, you lucky kid."

"Isn't she lovely?" Mom glowed.

P.J. gave a vicious jerk to his tie. "Step on it, Andie," he said between clenched teeth. "We've got a lot of people to pick up."

We picked up Rachel first since she lived right next door. She and I sat in the back seat together. "It's going to be fine," I whispered. "Don't worry. P.J.'s just a little bit ticked off about the change in the transportation arrangements. Don't let it get to you."

"Me? Ticked off?" P.J. said bitterly. "Heck, no. I love to get all dressed up and pay a fortune so I can play sardines in my own car."

Rachel smiled serenely.

I was impressed. I never dreamed she had such first-rate inner resources. For my part, I had a strong inclination to belt P.J. with the nearest blunt instrument.

Dooley's house was the next stop. His Jeep was sitting forlornly in the driveway, its tire impressively flat. I noticed with some relief that Dooley was wearing a white shirt and dress pants, even though he wasn't wearing a coat or tie. When he got in, a musky smell filled the car. I tried to back away from him, but it was not easy as the back seat was getting a tad crowded. Surreptitiously I reached over Rachel and opened the window a crack to dilute the smell, which was presumably Dooley's idea of a seductive scent. At least, I thought, the stench would help disguise the smell of liquor on Rachel's breath.

P.J. drove on to the Hamiltons'. He beeped and

Chris came bouncing out. Rachel looked out the window at him and heaved a deep sigh.

Chris threw open the car door and crawled into the back. I was relieved Rachel didn't fall out. "Want to sit on my lap, Rachel?" he suggested hopefully. "It's pretty crowded back here."

Rachel ended up getting on Chris's lap, and I got one of her coiled black braids right in my mouth when she turned her head to whisper in his ear.

"I can't believe this," P.J. said as he drove away. "Susie's going to think I'm a flipping bus driver. Jeez!"

Chris murmured something in Rachel's ear. She covered her mouth and giggled.

Dooley stared glumly out the window. I was too relieved that he hadn't put his arm around me to worry about him. I was just glad Mom wasn't there to see us stuffed into the back seat knee to chin. I hated to shatter her illusions, but even she would have to admit this was not exactly Cinderella's coach.

At Susie's house P.J. got out of the car. A few minutes later he came out holding Susie's hand and with a silly smile on his face. Susie's blond hair stood out on all sides as if she'd had a bad fright. She was dressed in pink with the kind of high heels podiatrists warn people against. She giggled when P.J. opened the front door for her. As soon as she got in the front seat, she turned around and looked at all of us. I guess she couldn't help but notice the tangled limbs in the back. "Y'all look awful crowded back there," she said. "Doesn't anybody want to come up here with us?"

P.J. turned around, lowered his eyebrows, and gave us a forbidding stare. We all said quickly that we were quite comfortable.

"Just get your elbow out of my rib, would you?" Chris said to me.

"Excuse me," I said politely.

"You sure?" Susie asked again.

We were quite sure.

Soon we were speeding away to the county agricultural building, which is where the dance was being held. "Did you hear the one about the guy who swallowed his pencil?" Susie said. "He said to his doctor, 'I just swallowed my pencil.' 'You swallowed your pencil?' his doctor says. 'Well, sit down and write your name.'" She giggled.

Beside me, Rachel burped.

"Did you eat any crackers?" I asked her in a hoarse whisper.

"Crackers?" she asked.

"Are you okay, Rachel?" I asked.

"Sure," she said.

Dooley nudged me. "Could you give me a little more space, Andie? I'm just about squashed."

I was just about squashed myself. I was actually almost to the point of asking Dooley to sit on my lap—it was that bad. Luckily, it wasn't terribly far to the county agricultural building.

Chris slid out of the back seat and held the door open for Rachel. When she got out, he put his arm around her solicitously. It was probably just as well. I was beginning to wonder whether she was capable of navigating under her own steam.

"Come on, Andie," said Dooley. He stuffed his hands in the pockets of his pants and began trotting toward the door. I ran to catch up with him.

Inside the building Rachel smiled beatifically at me. "My parents are chaperons," she said.

"They are?" I said absently. "That's wonderful." Frankly, I was beginning to wonder exactly how much Rachel was going to remember about this dream date.

The vast modern hall inside had been festooned with quantities of balloons. Swags of crepe paper adorned the ceiling, and a huge bouquet of hot-house lilies stood beside the punch bowl. A collection of small tables was lined up along each side of the hall where couples could sit when they weren't dancing. Ficus trees in huge pots stood between them to simulate forest greenery. Rachel's mother saw us when we came in and offered a friendly little wave.

"My parents aren't going to intrude on us," Rachel said to me solemnly. "They promised."

I put my hand on her shoulder and looked her right in the eye. "Rachel, are you all right?"

"Sure," she said.

The band was playing a slow tune, and Chris was watching the group with delight. "Aw-right!" He turned to Rachel. "Want to dance?"

"Sure," she said.

"What's going on with Rachel?" Dooley asked me after they'd gone. "She seems kind of weird."

I ignored the question. "Want to dance?" I asked brightly.

Dooley danced like a man carrying a ladder. This was not poetry in motion. "Love is a funny thing, isn't it?" he croaked.

"Ouch."

"Sorry." He removed his foot from my arch. "I mean, it just sort of hits you like a ton of bricks, and you can't do a thing about it."

"I wouldn't know, I'm afraid," I said primly. Nip it in the bud was my philosophy. I didn't like to stomp on Dooley's delicate feelings, but there were times when a person had to be cruel to be kind.

"Don't tell me," he said, "that you've never been in love!"

"No." I watched Rachel glide by me with a glazed smile. "Not that I'm complaining," I added hastily. "I'm willing to wait for the right guy to come along. I mean, I'll wait years, if necessary. I don't believe in getting involved in high school anyway."

"Yeah, but you've never even felt a little bit like, well, you know." His sallow skin darkened in what I supposed was a blush.

"Well, sure I've felt a little bit 'you know.'" I glanced over my shoulder at Rachel. "But never enough to make an absolute idiot of myself."

"Hey, don't worry about it." He punched my arm good-humoredly. "We all got to start somewhere."

Dooley and I sat out the next dance by mutual consent. I was not surprised when Rachel and Chris took the table next to ours when the band began a lively tune. If Rachel was up to fast dancing, I missed my guess.

"Hey, aren't those your parents, Rache?" Chris asked.

Mr. and Mrs. Green were making a stately promenade around the hall, nodding kindly at the young couples they passed.

"They won't intrude," Rachel assured us solemnly.

"Are you okay, Rachel?" Chris asked, worried. Chris didn't know Rachel well enough to know that silence and that spacey smile were not normal for her, but even he had begun to suspect something was wrong.

Mr. and Mrs. Green approached us at a regal pace and nodded at Rachel and Chris. Rachel gave *them* that serene smile. I decided that Chris's smile was a little forced, but the Greens didn't notice anything and glided on. Suddenly Rachel fell forward onto the table, her nose flat against its white enamel surface. Chris looked down on her in blank astonishment. "Je-rusalem!" he exclaimed.

A ficus tree blocked her parents' view of what had happened, but we were attracting curious stares from other dancers.

"I'm afraid she's been drinking," I whispered.

Dooley darted a quick glance around. "Come on, Chris. I'll help you get her outside."

It took Chris a second to grasp what Dooley was saying. "Oh," he said. "Yeah. Let's get her some fresh air. That's what she needs."

They put her arms around their necks and somehow managed to hustle her out the nearest fire exit without her mom and dad seeing. All that weight lifting they did turned out to have a practical application. I sat at the table smiling nervously at passing dancers. My mom was right, I reflected. Amazing things could happen at dances. Of course, this development was rather a strange twist on the old fairy tale. Cinderella turning into a pumpkin.

P.J. and Susie appeared suddenly. "What's going on?" asked P.J. "Somebody told me Rachel fainted."

"It must have been the heat," I said.

"What are you talking about, Andie? It's not hot in here."

"Rachel might have thought it was hot," said Susie. "Or maybe she's got the flu or something."

"Maybe that's it."

At last Dooley trailed back inside, his hands in his pockets, and a foolish smile on his face. He sat down beside me. "Do you know CPR?" he asked me.

I gasped. "You don't mean she's stopped breathing?"

"Keep it down, Andie. No, she's still breathing. It's just that we can't seem to bring her around."

"Golly, I wonder how much she had to drink." I realized now I should have found out where Rachel's dad's liquor cabinet was and then hidden the bottles. All of them.

The Greens were talking to some other chaperons over by a ficus tree in the corner. Amazingly, they didn't seem to have noticed anything.

Dooley and I sat in glum silence. "You think we'd better go out there and check on her?" I asked.

He shrugged. "I don't see what we can do."

A little later I heard the ambulance siren. I closed

my eyes as it got closer and closer. When it came to a screeching halt right outside the fire exit, Rachel's parents looked around the hall, startled. They came over to our table at once. "Andie," Mrs. Green asked, "has there been an accident? What is this ambulance about?"

"Uh, I don't really know much about it." I squirmed.

"I think we'd better go outside and check on this," she said. I cringed as the Greens pushed open the fire door and went outside.

There was no more siren, so I deduced that the ambulance attendants had decided this was no emergency. I felt reasonably certain, however, that neither Rachel nor Chris would rate it as the ideal dream date of all time.

Out on the dance floor the band played on.

Thirteen

"That was absolutely the worst time I've ever had in my life." Chris put his feet up on a kitchen chair. "And I'm counting when I broke my arm in the fourth grade. You should have seen the way those guys at the rescue squad looked at me. What could I do? I felt like I had to go in the ambulance with her. They kept asking me if she had taken any pills or anything, and I didn't know. I tried to explain it was the first time I'd ever been out with her." He shuddered. "Not to mention the last."

"Unreal," said P.J.

"Aw, come on," said Dooley. "It wasn't that bad."

Chris groaned. "And then when the Greens met us at the hospital! I thought Mrs. Green was going to die. She was the color of pea soup. I'm not kidding."

"How long were you over at the hospital?" asked P.J.

"I don't know. It seemed like forever. They pumped out Rachel's stomach or something gross like that. I just sat there in the emergency room trying to figure out if I should call my folks to come get me or ask the Greens for a ride home or what. Finally I called my dad. You talk about something that's hard to explain! I mean, I was just an innocent bystander, but everybody's treating me like the king of vice. I tell you, guys, I'm seriously thinking of giving up girls for good."

"Sure," said Dooley.

I was sitting unobtrusively in the leather recliner in the family room wondering what on earth I could have done to prevent the catastrophe.

I hadn't heard a word from Rachel since it had happened. I tried to call her Sunday, but I got Mrs. Green. She told me since Rachel was grounded she wasn't allowed to take calls from friends. I had no idea how Rachel was taking it. I could only guess. I felt the way people in a city must feel after an earthquake when the phone lines are down. It's like you know something bad has happened, but you don't have a full casualty list yet.

Belatedly, P.J. noticed me. "Hey, Andie, did you know Rachel had been drinking?"

I slipped down farther in the chair. "I noticed she had had a few when I went over to do her hair," I said. "I think she was trying to calm her nerves."

"I guess it worked," Dooley croaked.

P.J. stared at him.

"What did I do to deserve this?" complained

Chris. "Look, Andie, if any of your other girlfriends is a drunk, let me know now, huh? Give me a little warning. Golly, when I think of what I laid out for those tickets. Next time I'll save my money and just crawl a mile over broken glass. It'll be more fun."

"I had a really awful date a few weeks ago," P.J. said. "Myra Jenkins, remember? Allergic to seafood. She takes a bite of lobster Newburg and gets these pink patches all over her. She looked like a checkerboard. 'If you're allergic to the stuff, why did you eat it?' I said. 'I don't know,' she whines. And it was the most expensive thing on the menu too."

"Man, that's not in the same class at all." Chris shook his head. "You call that a bad date? It's not even first runner-up."

I got up and left. I couldn't stand it anymore. It really depressed me to think of what poor Rachel must be going through. And there the guys were sitting around and practically laughing about it. I went outside, sat on the fence, and looked up at the windows of Rachel's room. I was thinking I might be able to catch a glimpse of her if she was sitting on the bed watching for Chris the way she used to do. I figured it would be reassuring if I could just see her.

Suddenly she came to the window, pressed her nose against it, and gestured wildly.

"What?" I yelled.

She threw up the window and called down to me. "Meet me out back. I'm going to take out the garbage."

I waited for her out back by the Greens' garbage cans. The smell was oddly comforting. The world may fall apart, but some things are a constant. Like garbage.

A few minutes later Rachel came out carrying a limp plastic bag. Her eyes were red and swollen and her whole face looked puffy. She stuffed the garbage bag into the can and put the top on. "I'm grounded for the rest of my natural life," she said. Her nose sounded stuffed up.

"Golly, I'm sorry, Rache."

"We're going to 'reevaluate my sense of responsibility' in two months, and until then I have to come home straight after school and I can't even talk to anyone on the telephone!"

"That's tough," I said.

She clenched her fists. "I was so stupid. I can't believe I drank all that stuff! I mean, I guess I sort of lost track of how much I was drinking. I had no idea gin was so strong." Her violet eyes were watery. "I am so miserable, Andie. What is Chris saying?"

"Oh, about what you'd expect," I hedged.

"He never wants to see me again, does he?" she wailed. "I was so dumb, so stupid." She hit her fist against her head, then winced. "I have made such a fool of myself, I'll never live it down."

"Everybody makes mistakes."

"Not too many people make mistakes that get them grounded till Christmas," she said bitterly.

"Rachel!" yelled Mrs. Green. "How long can it take you to take out the garbage?"

"Coming!" she yelled. She banged the top of the

garbage can to lend verisimilitude to her claim. "They won't let me out of their sight. I'm a prisoner. My every movement is watched, and tomorrow the furniture store delivers a liquor cabinet that has a dead bolt lock. As if I would ever touch the stuff again. My only comfort is that someday this experience will make an extremely bleak little short story that will probably get me an A in creative writing. It will be full of existential angst and despair. I think I'll call it 'Degradation.'"

"Rachel? What on earth are you doing out there?" yelled Mrs. Green.

Rachel shot me a hopeless look, then turned and trudged back to her house.

Well, at least she seemed to be taking it better than she took the loss of her hat.

At school on Monday when I didn't see Rachel at lunch, I was a little worried. I finished eating quickly and went off to check under the stairs at A wing. I knew that was where she had taken her apple and sandwich before when she had been trying to avoid Chris.

I heard her talking as I approached the stairs, her characteristic helter-skelter syllables tumbling over one another.

"Rachel?" I bent down and peeked under the stairs.

"Hi, Andie." She was under the stairs, all right. She flashed me a bright smile.

"Hi," croaked Dooley.

I jumped. Then I saw him in the darkness beyond Rachel, sitting a little awkwardly. He had to bend his head some to fit under the stairs there. I recalled that Dooley hadn't been at lunch, either. I hadn't even wondered where he was. I guess my chief feeling when he hadn't shown up had been sheer relief.

"Since I'm grounded till Christmas," Rachel said, "I have to squeeze in my social life wherever I can. Dooley's sharing my peanut butter sandwich."

"That's good," I said. I backed off a little. "Well, I just wanted to check on you and make sure you were all right, that's all."

"I'm telling Dooley about Mandelbrot's theories of chaos as a principle in the universe. You see, when a system gets overloaded, you get chaos, but even the chaos has a pattern. It's like there's some kind of principle underlying it." Rachel considered her sandwich with a frown. "I feel like that sort of applies to my life. I mean, just when everything is totally a mess, things start to get clearer."

"It's real interesting, the theories and all," echoed Dooley.

"Right," I said. "Well, see ya. I mean, I'll be seeing you both, uh, later."

Dooley and Rachel? Of course, when I thought about it, I realized they did have something in common. Their housekeeping habits for starters.

I glanced at my watch. There were ten minutes left in my lunch period. I had gulped down only a few bites of my food before going to find Rachel. Now it was pretty obvious she didn't need me. I walked to the small building where they kept the vending machines, over near the breezeway. I got myself a candy bar, then perched on the steps and unwrapped my chocolate, meditating on the weirdness of life. Rachel and Dooley? Well, why not?

The vending machine clunked behind me, and I looked around. Pete Joyner smiled a little shamefaced. "They just don't give you enough lunch at this place. I came to get some dessert."

"You don't have to explain to me," I said. Now that I wasn't worried about Rachel, my appetite had returned full force. I hadn't eaten much lately. I had some catching up to do.

I could hear the sound of confused voices as the cafeteria door opened and closed. People were coming out from lunch. I continued placidly chewing my candy bar. Maybe it showed that I was getting to be an old hand at Westmarket High, but now I was prepared to eat a candy bar in less than three minutes. Lunch period was almost over, and I wasn't a bit worried.

Pete sat down next to me. "Somebody told me you went to the dance with Dooley."

I shuddered. It would be a long time before I could think of that dance without getting chills. "I did."

"Is he your boyfriend?"

"Good grief, no! What made you think that?"

"I just thought since you went to the dance with him and all."

"A favor to a friend. Purely." I didn't want to go into the grisly details.

Pete poured his package of M & M's down his throat. He licked his lips and crumbled the package in his fist. "Candy bars keep getting littler. Have you noticed that?"

I hadn't actually. It seemed to me that they had gotten bigger. But I could imagine that when Pete Joyner was having a growth spurt, it must seem like everything in the world was getting littler.

"How tall is your dad, Pete?"

He thought about it. "Six five, I think."

"And your mom?"

He grinned. "Five eleven. My family figures I'm still growing." He struggled to his feet. "I think I'll just get another one since these are so little."

I was still sitting when Chris and P.J. suddenly rounded the corner of the building.

"Andie!" whooped Chris. "There you are!"

"Why'd you run off from lunch like that?" asked P.J. " 'Bet she's sneaking off to meet Dooley,' I said to Chris. 'Let's go find them.' "

They both grinned at me. "Where is he?" asked P.J.

"Yeah, we heard a guy talking, didn't we, P.J.? Can't have you two sneaking off to make out by the vending machines, can we?"

"Absolutely not!" P.J. chimed in. " 'What those two need,' I said to Chris, 'is chaperons!' So here we are!"

I glared. They were trying to drive me crazy, and they were doing it on purpose.

I heard the vending machine clunk behind me. Then I felt rather than saw Pete Joyner's presence behind me blocking the doorway. "Hi, guys," he rumbled.

They looked up at him in confusion.

Pete sat down next to me and began deliberately unwrapping his Snickers bar.

I put my hand on Pete's knee. This almost caused him to drop his candy, but P.J. and Chris were so mesmerized by his sudden appearance that they didn't notice his surprise. "I'm sorry I had to rush off from lunch," I cooed. "But it's so hard for Pete and me to get any time together alone."

Chris turned pink and nudged P.J. with his foot. "Let's go," he muttered.

"See you guys later," said Pete amiably.

Chris and P.J. didn't stand on ceremony, but turned speedily and left.

Pete and I sat in companionable silence while he devoured the chewy nugget. At last he pulled out a handkerchief the size of a peace flag and patted his lips. He smiled at me. "You really scared me when you touched me like that, but I figured I'd just go along with you. Trying to give P.J. a hard time, huh?"

I looked at him in surprise. I hadn't noticed before that he had kind, brown eyes. I've always had a weakness for brown eyes.

"Not entirely," I said.

"Huh?"

"I mean, I wasn't *only* trying to give them a hard time," I said. I was remembering how Pete kept wanting to have more study dates, how he had asked me if I was going to the Falling Leaves Dance. It had been a last-minute thought, to be sure, but didn't it show that he was sort of interested in me?

All at once I made up my mind. Pete liked me, and the guys were terrified of him. This relationship could have a real future.

"Want to split a candy bar?" Pete asked. "I don't think I could eat a whole one."

"Sure," I said, noticing with pleasure the little flecks of gold in his big brown eyes. "I'd absolutely *love* to."

———————————

To find out what happens next to Andie, look for *Dooley MacKenzie Is Totally Weird*, coming in February 1991.